The Magical Mrs. Iptweet and Me

Winner of New Mexico Discovery Award
2006/2nd Place/Fiction

"Mrs. Iptweet is a refreshing eccentric.... who reminds us that dreaming big is always in season. Barbara Mayfield remembers what the wonder and discovery of nine years old is like."
– Jonathan Richards, journalist, actor, cartoonist, illustrator

"*The Magical Mrs. Iptweet and Me* is full of original characters with voices not heard elsewhere in literature for the young at heart: a nine-and-a-half year old Budding Cartographer, a Recycling Cowgirl Artist, a Classical Banjo Player, and, of course the magical Mrs. Iptweet, part Earth Mother, part Good Witch. Like Prudence, while reading I often "felt a giggle start to happen in me" and longed to get out my glitter pens or work on Tapping the Power of the Earth. But this story also has a serious side and there are great lessons in it about dealing with grief, loss, fear, and divorce in creative and nurturing ways...."
– Jenice Gharib, Former Director of the Southwest Literary Center

".... a little bit of Mrs. Iptweet lives inside all of us – the desire to help a child grow up strong and independent."
– Jennifer Owings Dewey, Author/Illustrator, Orbis Pictus Award winner, Spur Juvenile Non-fiction Award.

"This is a must have.... I wish Mrs. Iptweet lived on my street!"
– Janeen Mason, Author/Illustrator, *Ocean Commotion: Sea Turtles!*, Winner of the US Maritime Literature Award

The Magical Mrs. Iptweet and Me

written and illustrated by
Barbara Mayfield

AZRO PRESS, SANTA FE · 2009

ISBN 10: 1-929115-18-0
ISBN 13: 978-1-929115-18-1
Library of Congress Control Number: 2008940202
Copyright © 2009 by Barbara Mayfield

Book designed by Marcy Heller
Fonts used include Adobe Caslon Pro, Cali ITCTT,
Handwriting-Dakota, and Kid Type Marker

Printed in the United States of America by Paper Tiger
in Santa Fe, New Mexico

This book has been printed in full compliance with
the US Consumer Product Safety Improvement Act (CPSIA).

For Modesta

CHAPTER ONE
Blah-ville

It was another boring day in my boring life and I wasn't
even ten yet. I came home from school and my mom was taking a nap. Her job as bookkeeper at the bookkeeping company
is an early-bird job. This means she is sleepy in the afternoon
when I come home from the Dullest School in the World. Her
nap means I have to be quiet, quiet, and quiet. I am nine-and-
a-half and being quiet is not my style. There was nothing to do
but leave our boring house in search of some excitement.

Except that our street is extremely boring, too. It's called
Durham Street, as in DOOR HAM. I wish big, smart, snorty
pigs lived on our street and answered the doors when I knock.
That would be interesting, and our street's name would make
sense. But snorty pigs never answer the doors around here. On
that dreary day in the month of March, I couldn't take the
blahness any longer. I decided it was time for Drastic Action.

I said to myself, "Self, it's time to walk to the Corner Market and watch some crimes being committed."

I quietly put on my blue sweater. I quietly closed the front door, and quietly tiptoed down our steps to the sidewalk. I scuffed to the corner to cross our street. I always remember to look both ways, since my mom would be really upset if I got run over. I looked to my left, down my street. No cars were coming. I saw the houses and the trees, all in rows.

So far, the most interesting things about my street are the trees. They are tall and wide. They live between the sidewalk and the curb, two long rows of big tree-ness on both sides of the street. Their name is Maple. The maple trees on my street are extremely leafy in the summer. They have bare arms in the winter. Winter is the dull time, so that is when I spy on the

Maple in summer   Maple in winter

birds' nests and mark their location on my maps.

On one of his visits, my dad showed me how to draw a map. He said I should start small, so I made a map of my bedroom. I drew a rectangle first, and then pretended I was looking at my room from above. I imagined I was glued onto the ceiling.

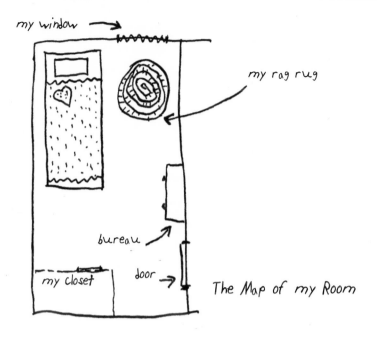

my window →

my rag rug

bureau

my closet   door →

The Map of my Room

Then I drew in my bed, bureau, the window, my door, the closet and my rag rug. My Gran Modesta braided real rags into a cozy, circle-shape rug just for me. When my Gran was still alive, she and I sat on my special rug and read stories together. My Gran and I liked adventure stories, especially exotic stories from foreign lands. We read from the dictionary, too, because Gran believed that words are adventures all by themselves.

I also drew onto my map my bumpy pink bedspread and the silky, heart-shaped pillow from my Aunt Belle. This pillow is full of interesting smelly leaves and twigs from the desert.

My Aunt Belle lives in the Southwest. It is all desert there. Aunt Belle is a Professional Recycling Cowgirl Artist. This means she collects interesting objects that have been squished up, stomped on, or run over. Most people think of these objects as trash. Aunt Belle attaches them together in an artistic way, always with a western theme.

Personally, I think Aunt Belle is living an interesting life.

My mom thinks Aunt Belle's career is unsanitary, so I am not allowed to pick up trash off the street to send to her, no matter how artistic it is. I promised to wear gloves and put the smashed-up stuff right into a plastic bag so that no part of the artistic trash comes into contact with any part of my body, but still the answer is No. This is another reason why my life is so dull.

After I looked down the street to my left, I looked to my right. I was glad I did because a gigantic old purple truck was barreling down the side street. I waited on the corner for it to pass, but instead, the truck slowed down and stopped in the middle of the street in front of me. The driver man rolled down his window and leaned out of his noisy purple truck.

"Hey there, Young Lady, what is the name of this street?" he yelled at me.

I used my loud voice and yelled, "Durham Street, Sir."

I heard him say to his passenger man, "Did you hear that, Bob? This is Durham Street. All righty-rooney."

Then the driver man yelled back to me, "Thank you kindly, Miss," and tipped his baseball cap to me. He rolled up his window and put on his turn signal. He turned right onto my street.

I never saw a purple truck turn onto Durham Street before. Who are these guys, I wondered? What are they doing here? Maybe something interesting is going to happen on Durham Street. The last time a few moments of excitement happened around here was last summer.

Last summer at number four-o-two, Mrs. Romero's parakeet, Señora Puff o' Fluff, escaped. It flew right out the front door and perched on the branch of an azalea bush. There was a big hubbub, but then Mr. Miller of number four-o-four caught Señora Puff o' Fluff in his bare hands. He offered Señora Puff o' Fluff a piece of banana, and that was that. Our street went back to blahness.

If I ever escape from here, it will take more than a piece of fruit to get me back.

Bird in cage

I watched the big interesting truck crawl slowly down our narrow street. But the truck did not stop. It kept going to the very end. Then its turn signal started blinking and the truck turned right onto the the busy street, gone forever. I sat down on the curb. What's the use, I thought.

I wish my dad still lived around here.

On his last visit, my dad said I did a good job on my bedroom map, and that even though I am only nine-and-a-half, I am a Budding Cartographer. My dad is a Classical Banjo Player. My dad uses maps a lot in his career, to get from one playing gig to another. That way he does not have to ask anyone for directions. My mom says it's a guy thing, not asking for directions.

My dad's dream is to become a World Famous Banjo Player and give solo banjo concerts at Carnegie Hall. He says the banjo is seriously underestimated in big-time music circles, and he hopes to live long enough to see it be properly appreciated.

My dad's banjo

In the meantime, he is doing his part to spread the Joy of Banjo by playing at dances, weddings, and parades. I myself have never been to a dance, wedding, or parade. My mom says I am not old enough yet to handle the excitement. I think my mom is wrong about this.

I admire my dad for his dedication to fine art music, but I wish he would visit me more. I miss eating breakfast at 7:30 a.m. every single day with my dad. Since he and my mom split up, he is traveling to many interesting places to advance his career. And, besides that, I have a new map to show him. After I made my bedroom map, I made a map of my street. To draw my map, I pretended I was floating in the sky above my street and looking down. I drew fluffy circles onto my map where the trees are located. Then I drew shapes for the houses. I marked each house number and the neighbors' names that I know. If I didn't know who lived there, I marked down a large orange question mark, or whatever color I felt like using.

The house at number four-o-six is empty. No one has lived there for a long time. I marked a black X on it, because it looks kind of spooky. I used a blue pencil to mark down where the pets live. Dog. Cat. Pig. Ha ha. I marked down each bird nest and lavender plant with my purple pencil.

My Gran Modesta had a thing for lavender. Lavender was her favorite plant, color, and smell. So far there is only one lavender plant on my street; it's in a pot on our front porch. My mom and I dug it up from Gran's garden after Gran passed on.

To add some excitement to my street map, I marked where the sewer drains are, and any especially large sidewalk cracks. My mom says that the big gnarly maple tree roots have caused these cracks, but I think the cause could be mini-earthquakes or tectonic plate-shifting. My mom says that we don't live in an earthquake zone, but in case she is wrong about this, I measure the width of the cracks each week. If I detect any sudden changes, or if there are any big earth-moving events, I will alert the neighborhood. I have marked these exciting danger zones on my map in red pencil.

I sat on the curb for a few minutes. If only my neighborhood

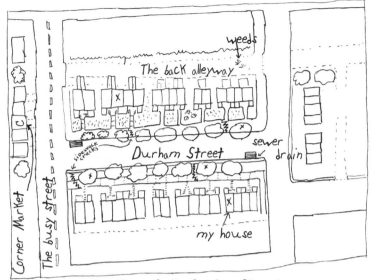

The Map of My Boring Street

was full of Wild Parakeets, Talking Pigs, and Earthquakes, I'd never be bored. But no. Ordinary people answer the doors, the birds are in their cages, and the ground is perfectly still. Ho hum, ho hum.

I stood up and brushed off the back of my pants. The coast was clear so I crossed our street and turned down the back alleyway toward the creepy creepiness of the Corner Market.

I have always been suspicious of the Corner Market. The Corner Market is located in the middle of the block, so its name is a big fat lie. I think the Corner Market is a front for something nasty. The owner guy, Big Nick, is short. Big Nick's grown-up son, Little Nick, is tall. The two Nicks cut coupons from stacks of newspapers, then claim the coupons as if customers bought stuff.

My Aunt Belle told me that doing this is totally illegal; it is a way they make money.

At the top of the back alley I scanned the ground for any trash art that I wouldn't pick up. Nothing but dirt, scraggly

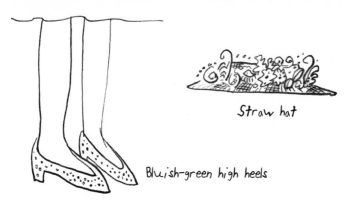

Straw hat

Bluish-green high heels

weeds and concrete. I looked up and guess what? The mysterious purple truck was parked at the other end of the alleyway! It must have turned off the busy street right into the back alleyway. Oh, wow, I thought, excitement is happening.

Maybe it's a robbery. The driver man was friendly, though, and he was not wearing a mask. Maybe they are FBI guys in disguise and are searching for spies or criminals on Durham Street. But I have not seen any suspicious-looking people around. Or maybe it is a fancy moving truck. Maybe new people are moving into the empty, spooky house. I hope they have a kid my age or at least a snorty pig to play with. Ha ha.

I saw a lady standing in the driveway near the mysterious truck. She was staring at a sorry-looking patch of dirt. I walked on down the alleyway towards the lady and the grapey-color truck.

I didn't know it then, but my life was about to change forever.

When I got close, the lady turned around and said, "Hello there, Youthful One." And then she went back to staring at the patch of dirt.

I said, "Hello," and stared at her.

Her skirt was bright orange and billowy. Her blousy top was yellow, with a mountain painted on it. On her feet were bluish-green high heels with tiny polka dots cut out, so I could see rosy pink leather underneath. And on her head was a large straw hat, with a million silk flowers and papier mâché birds nesting all the way around the brim. Under her hat, I saw her flaming red curly hair. Wow, I thought, this lady looks like a party.

I knew I ought to stop staring at the lady, so I stared at her patch of dirt. It sort of looked like the other pathetic patches of dirt poking out between the concrete slabs of the alleyway, but hers was worse. Her dirt was covered with gravel and stones. I wondered if she was a gardener. Probably her day is ruined because nothing ever grows in the boring dirt around here except dumb weeds.

The back of #406 Durham Street

Gravel and stones

The lady stopped staring at the gravel and stones. She took a deep breath, looked at me and smiled. She said, "So, Young One, are you one of my new neighbors?"

I said, "Yes, ma'am."

"And where do you live?" the lady asked me.

"Across the street at the other end, ma'am," I said. "Our house has a lavender plant in a pot on the porch."

"Lavender is a lovely plant and a powerful herb."

"Yeah. And it has a good smell, too."

"Yes, it does," said the lady. Then she asked me, "Have you lived here a long time, Young Miss?"

"Yes, ma'am, my whole entire life."

"And how long would that be?"

"Nine-and-a-half years, ma'am."

"And how is your life going so far, Youngster Gal?"

I didn't answer the lady right away. I had never really thought about how my life was going. It just seemed to go by itself.

I said, "Um, great. Really good. It's okay, I guess, but I get bored sometimes."

The lady's eyes got all bright and sparkly. She looked right at me and said, "Ah, yes, boredom."

"I am a Budding Cartographer, though." I told the new lady about my bedroom map and my map of the street. She said my maps sounded very interesting.

Then she asked, "Do you know anything about gardening, Miss Girl?"

I said, "Um, well, my Gran was a gardener."

"Oh, you have a grandmother?"

"Yes. But she died," I said.

"Oh, I'm so sorry to hear that," the lady said.

"Yeah," I said. "I miss my Gran. So does my mom."

"Oh, I am sure."

"My mom still gets sad a lot. And grumpy, too."

"It takes some time to get used to life without a loved one," the lady said.

"Yeah, it's taking really long," I said. "Usually my mom is only in a bad mood when my dad blows into town to take me out for a quick visit. But since Gran has gone to her Reward, my mom is in a mood a lot."

The lady nodded her head. She said in a quiet voice, "It's understandable, but not easy."

I said, "But my friend Bea Bea's mom says soon my mom will be feeling better."

"I am certain that is true." The lady smiled at me. I looked at her patch of dirt.

"So, do you know anything about gardening, Miss Girl?" the lady asked me again.

I said, "My mom says the dirt around here is too stressed-out to grow anything special. Just weeds and trees can take the city air. My mom doesn't let me water Gran's lavender plant. No, ma'am, I don't know anything about gardening."

The lady said, "Great! I wonder if you would you consider assisting me in Tapping the Power of the Ground?"

I said, "Huh? Okay. Sure. But I don't really know what that is."

"That's wonderful," she said. "We'll start as soon as I have settled in. Please call me Mrs. Iptweet."

"Mrs. Iptweet. Um, okay," I said. What a weird and cheerful name, I thought. Like a kind of bird or a fancy cracker.

Mrs. Iptweet asked, "What shall I call you?"

Out of my mouth, all by itself, came "Sheherazade."

CHAPTER TWO

Why Did I Say That?

Why did I say my name was Sheherazade? Sheherazade is not my real name. My real name is a dreary and dull name – a terrible name for a girl who likes adventure and excitement like me. But Sheherazade, the exotic storyteller lady in Arabia, had a great name, a truly great name. Gran and I read a lot about the interesting lady Sheherazade. Probably the name Sheherazade means Brave Adventure Girl or Miss Ultra Amazing in Greek or Persian, or some other mysterious foreign language. So far I only speak one language.

Mrs. Iptweet said, "It's nice to meet you, Sheherazade."

Then I heard the sound of big feet stomping around inside the purple truck. The driver man and his passenger guy climbed out of the back of the truck.

Mrs. Iptweet said, "Sheherazade, please meet Mr. Bob and Mr. Darryl. They are skilled experts in their field."

Mr. Bob and Mr. Darryl wore bright orange jumpsuits with purple embroidered patches. Their patches said Relocation Engineers Unlimited. Mr. Bob took off his green hat and bowed to me from the waist like a prince. Mr. Darryl put two fingers onto the edge of his cap and winked. I said, "Hey," and stuck my hands in my jeans pockets, because I don't know what else to do when people bow and wink.

Mrs. Iptweet said that my name, Sheherazade, was a very interesting name. She decided on calling me Zaady or Chérie for short, because variety is the spice of life. Chérie means Dear One in the French language. I said that those nicknames would be fine with me.

Mrs. Iptweet said, "Okey dokey, Zaady Gal."

I thought Mrs. Iptweet was pretty funny. I felt a giggle start to happen in me.

Then Mr. Bob said, "Well, Darryl, my man, shall we fulfill our destiny for today?"

Mr. Darryl said, "Absolutely, my friend. Let us prepare."

Mr. Bob and Mr. Darryl stretched and flexed their muscles and began the parade of boxes into Mrs. Iptweet's new house. All the boxes were labeled in blue glitter letters. The first box out of the van said HAMMOCKS. The next box said DANCING SHOES.

Then WIGS.

Then PUPPETS.

Then MAGIC WANDS.

Then DOLLS.

Then GLITTER.

Then finally, FEATHERS and TWINKLE LIGHTS.

I wished I could open up the boxes and see the dolls and wigs and puppets and glitter and magic wands and everything else right away, but more stuff was being carried out of the big purple truck.

A Secret Code

Mr. Darryl lifted a large, heavy trunk. It was dark blue leather, with a mermaid and seashells painted on it. This trunk was inscribed with a Secret Code: H-2-O. I will crack this code as soon as I can.

I volunteered to carry two small wooden boxes because I wanted to see the inside of Mrs. Iptweet's new house. The gold letters on these small boxes said: DIVINATION–TAROT–RUNES. I did not know what the words meant, but I like mysterious words.

I followed the moving guys into the car-smelling garage and then into the basement, which was pretty dark and smelled like wet stones. The rickety rackety basement stairway led up into a closet. We walked through the closet into the sunny, warm dining room and then into the shady, cool living room. In the living room I stepped up two steps onto a landing and followed the flight of sturdy stairs to the second floor all by myself.

Mrs. Iptweet asked me to put the two mysterious boxes into her meditation-room-to-be, the middle-sized room. Naturally, I had to check out all the rooms in order to know the sizes. Here is my report on the upstairs area: the biggest room is pretty big and in the front of the house. The walls in there are covered with blue wallpaper, flowery and flaky. I found a tiny bathroom in the hallway between the big bedroom and the two smaller rooms. The skylight in the bathroom lets a lot of brightness in, so I could see the broken tiles really easily. One of the small rooms in the back of the house is extremely small. The room right next to it is medium small, so I knew that this was the meditation-room-to-be. The walls of these two rooms are painted Disgust-o-Green.

It's hard for me to imagine a person like Mrs. Iptweet living in such a grim, ugly house. She seems lively and perky to me, even grimness-free. Maybe she will call in some Redecoration Engineers.

Very carefully, I placed the mystery boxes on the floor of the middle-sized room, the meditation-room-to-be. I looked out the big window in that small room and saw the rooftops and antennas and the tallest treetops in my neighborhood. I leaned over the windowsill and looked straight down. There was Mrs. Iptweet and the purple moving truck in the alleyway, looking smaller than usual.

I said, "Yoo-hoo, Mrs. Iptweet." And waved.

Mrs. Iptweet looked up and smiled and waved back at me. I could see that Mr. Bob had started on a batch of baskets, so I scooted downstairs as fast as I could. I did not want to miss anything.

The baskets were labeled in glued-on red sequins: STAMPS–INK–BRUSHES–PENS–COLORED PENCILS. Mr. Bob carried these baskets into the garage because this is where Mrs. Iptweet's studio will be. I could hardly stand the excitement. Art supplies! A person can make a lot of great stuff with art supplies, especially with colored pencils.

I called to Mrs. Iptweet, "Mrs. Iptweet, I have colored pencils, too. I have a red, an orange, a green, a blue, a yellow, a purple, a black and a brown pencil. Are you an artist, Mrs. Iptweet? My best pen has blue ink. I use it to make maps. I could show you how to make a map, Mrs. Iptweet. Guess what else? My Aunt Belle is an artist, too. She is a trash artist, so she uses a lot of glue and rust, but no pencils. I could show you how to draw a map, and if you wanted, we could try out your colored pencils, Mrs. Iptweet. I bet they would work great."

I had to stop talking and take a breath.

Mrs. Iptweet put down her basket and said, "Yes, Zaady Gal, I am an artist. You must show me, at the earliest opportunity, how to make a map. And yes, let's use my pencils. No problem."

I will definitely show Mrs. Iptweet my map of the neighborhood. Because she is new around here, my map could be a very big help to her. But first I will erase the big black X on house number four-o-six. I will write in the words MRS. IPTWEET in blue ink.

I didn't think the afternoon could get any better, but I was wrong. Next, the Mister Guys carried in Mrs. Iptweet's furniture. Mr. Darryl brought a wooden rocking chair out of the truck. At first, I thought it was just an ordinary rocking chair, but when Mr. Darryl carried it out of the dark into the sunlight I saw that the rocking chair was definitely not ordinary. It was painted all over in hearts and spiral shapes, and curvy lines and dots. It was not ordinary neat painting. It was Wild Painting.

Mrs. Iptweet noticed my eyes, which get very wide open when I am surprised or shocked.

She said, "Sheherazade, this is the chair in which I rocked my first-born son, and then my second-born son. I thought it was important for them to feel welcome in the world, and to experience a festive atmosphere as soon as possible."

Mrs. Iptweet told me that now her baby sons are grown-up men. Her older son is a Chef and a Married Man. Her younger son is a Geographer, an expert at telling people where they are. So they are much older than nine-and-a-half. Darn.

The next thing out of the purple van was Mrs. Iptweet's bed. It was a huge bed, made out of actual trees. Curly vines curled up the bare tree trunks and branches and made a curly canopy. I wished I had a bed like that. It would be like sleeping in the woods without all the fuss and muss. My mom does not like fuss and muss.

Mrs. Iptweet said it is a good bed for dreaming. Mrs. Iptweet probably has great, exciting dreams. I never have great, exciting dreams, and I've never been to a wedding, a dance, or a parade either, and there is nothing to do around here.

I heard my mother calling me. She has a voice that travels a whole city block when she wants it to. I said good-bye to Mr. Bob and Mr. Darryl.

Then I said, "Bye, Mrs. Iptweet. Uh, when do I come by to help you with the, um, Power Tapping stuff?"

Mrs. Iptweet smiled at me and said, "I will contact you very soon, Sheherazade. Keep an eye out for my message."

She waved goodbye as I walked up the alleyway.

On my way home I had a lot of thoughts and questions in my mind. Will I need a special outfit to Tap for Power? Will it hurt? Mrs. Iptweet didn't seem like a hurty type of person. How long will it take her to settle into her new house? What kind of a message will she send? Maybe a message in the mail, like my Aunt Belle sends. I like to get mail, especially oddball mail from my Aunt Belle.

I wondered if I could fit a tree into my bedroom. Would my mom mind? If I am quiet when I drag it up the stairs, maybe she won't notice. When will it be polite for me to ask to use some of Mrs. Iptweet's colored pencils on my maps? I wonder

if she has any sparkle pens. Oh, sparkle pens would look so great on my maps.

All of a sudden I was home, sniffing the air for dinner smells. I remembered that I never did watch the coupon-cutting crimes being committed at the Corner Market that day. And I didn't mind at all.

CHAPTER THREE

I Wait and Wait

The days dragged by. Every day seemed like a year since I didn't hear from Mrs. Iptweet.

My mom said, "A watched pot never boils." That means do something interesting while you are waiting.

So I read books. I measured the sidewalk cracks – no changes. I colored in the houses on my map of our street. One night I filled up a pot with water, turned on the stove and watched it for a long time until my mom came into the kitchen. She turned off the flame, and said, "Darling Girl, you are a nut. Here, wash these tomatoes, we are making Chicken Fiesta tonight."

After four days of waiting, there was nothing left to do. I went to my room, and sat on my rag rug, the rug that Gran made for me. I twiddled my thumbs for awhile. I looked around my room. Plain old white curtains with pink pom-poms on the edges. Plain old pink bureau with clothes sticking out of the drawers. Plain old bed covered with the bumpy pink bedspread. Ho hum.

Then an idea came to me. A great idea. No, a truly great idea. I thought, while I am waiting around for Mrs. Iptweet to get settled into her new house, I'll make a tree bed! A tree bed like Mrs. Iptweet's. Once I start Tapping the Power of the Ground with Mrs. Iptweet, I will be much too busy to make a fancy tree bed. I'll have interesting dreams and an exciting life when I make my own kid-sized dreaming bed, my very own Dream-o-rama. Wow!

I heard my mom's voice calling me from the foot of the stairs.

She said, "I could use a hand down here."

I had a lot of bounciness in me from having the good idea, so I ran down the stairs loud and fast to peel the carrots. I talked to my mom about my math test and about her math work at the bookkeeping company. I did not mention anything about my newest brilliant Dream-o-rama idea.

The next day, Bea Bea and I walked home from school together like usual. When we got to the edge of the Leafy Park Woods, I told Bea Bea my Dream-o-rama idea. My friend Bea Bea is shorter than me and has strawberry blonde hair. We have been friends since first grade.

I said, "Here is my plan, Bea Bea. We collect fallen-down tree branches from right here in the Leafy Park Woods. That way we won't need a ladder or a chain saw, which we do not have. I will sneak the branches past my mom into my room. Look, here is a branch on the ground right now."

I picked up the gnarly old branch. Bea Bea looked at me funny.

"Don't worry, Bea Bea," I said. "We can have sleep-overs and I'll let you sleep in the Dream-o-rama sometimes."

I shook some of the dirt off the dead branch. My friend Bea Bea rolled her eyes up into her head. When her

Leafy Park Woods

eyes came back down again she said, "You are crazy, Girl. Don't you know that all kinds of bugs live in fallen-down, dead tree branches?"

I looked at the branch in my hand. Bea Bea made her hand into a spidery shape and squiggled her hand up my arm.

"The bugs will come out at night and crawl all over you. Yee-hah-hah-ha," she said.

I dropped the branch fast. My whole body did a shudder and I choked. I jumped away from Bea Bea's spider hand and the bug-infested tree branch. I thought, Bea Bea is right. Even fake bugs crawling on my body freak me out. I do not want to wake up screaming from scary girl-eating monster insect dreams. I decided not to use bug-infested dead wood to make my Dream-o-rama.

What else could I use, I asked myself, to make a great fancy Dream-o-rama bed? I tapped my lip with my pointing finger and looked around the woods. The answer was right there on the ground in the creek bed. Rocks. I like rocks. Rocks are interesting. Rocks live near trees, but bugs do not live in rocks.

"What about rocks, Bea Bea?" I asked.

Bea Bea said, "Yeah, rocks would work. There is a good-looking rock right over there."

So each day, on the way home from the Dull Dull Dull School, with Bea Bea at my side, I searched in the creek bed for a really great, big rock. And every day, I found one. The rocks were heavy in my backpack, but I am very strong.

It was no problem at all tiptoeing upstairs past my napping mom with a big rock in my backpack each day. After I put each rock under my bed, I tiptoed back downstairs to search for Mrs. Iptweet's special message to me about Tapping the Power of the Ground.

But nothing, nowhere.

Even after thirteen days, when I had thirteen big smooth round rocks hanging out in the dark under my bed, there was still no note from Mrs. Iptweet. Maybe Mrs. Iptweet was kidding me about Tapping the Power of the Ground, I thought. What does it mean anyway? I'm just a kid, and maybe she doesn't really care about kids, except for her own grown-up sons. Maybe she forgot about me.

The next day, I didn't look for a dumb old message from Mrs. Iptweet. I didn't look in the mailbox, or under the garden rocks. I didn't look under the porch sofa cushions either. I gave up on Mrs. Iptweet. Oh well, I thought, at least I have a lot of rocks under my bed, and big plans about what to do with them. Who needs Mrs. Iptweet anyway?

After school, I scuffed up the steps to our porch and headed over to plop down on the porch sofa. But I tripped over the lavender pot. Someone had moved it over a little bit. But who?

Then I saw it, a triangle of white, sticking out from underneath the pot. It was paper! It was a note! It was a secret note written in sparkly ink just for me! I felt all tingling inside. The secret note read:

Dear Sheherazade,
It's time. Let's begin.
At your earliest convenience,
Mrs. Iptweet

The secret note

I scooted inside to put my books down as quietly as I could. I did not want to wake up my mom. I crept outside again. Then I ran, ran, ran, as fast as I could across the street and down the alleyway to the back of Mrs. Iptweet's house. I am a fast runner.

Mrs. Iptweet was outside looking down at the pathetic dirt.

I said, "Hi, Mrs. Iptweet. I found your message. Now is my earliest convenience, okay? What do I do?"

"It's good to see you, Sheherazade," Mrs. Iptweet said. "Thank you for your patience."

"Sure, Mrs. Iptweet, you're welcome," I gasped. I was breathing hard from my fast running. "What do we do first, Mrs. Iptweet, to Tap the Power of the Ground?"

"Let's look things over for a moment, Sheherazade."

Mrs. Iptweet and I looked over the rocky stones covering the stressed-out dirt. It was a terrible sight.

I said, "This situation looks pretty serious to me, Mrs. Iptweet. Maybe we should use dynamite. Dynamite will get rid of these stones pretty fast."

"Mmmm. No dynamite, Chérie," said Mrs. Iptweet. "Too noisy. Besides, I have a plan."

I began to learn about the Power of the Ground that very afternoon. It turns out that Mrs. Iptweet believes in Dirt and its Inherent Power.

"Don't be fooled by dead-looking dirt, Chérie," Mrs. Iptweet said. "In what looks like not much lies mighty and delightful treasure. First, we move the stones."

Mrs. Iptweet handed me a pink trowel and a green and white striped plastic bucket, into which I put my scooped-up stones. Mrs. Iptweet put on her polka-dot gloves and pushed stones into a metal kitchen bowl. We scooped and scooped about a hundred times or more. The stones were all different colors: solid gray, speckled gray and brown, pearly white, green, pink, gold, and black. Like tiny pieces of my Dream-o-rama creek rocks.

When the ground was almost bare, we used our fingers to gather up every single stony stone. We made a tidy pyramid of gravel on the driveway. The pile was as high as my knees.

Then Mrs. Iptweet scooped up a handful of dirt.

She said, "Chérie, let's take a sniff and see what we've got here."

We put our noses next to the crumbly darkness and breathed in the smell. It smelled like dirt to me. Mrs. Iptweet studied the dirt very carefully. Her eyes opened wide and she got all excited.

"Sheherazade, look here. A worm. I see a worm in this handful."

I looked. Yes. There was a huge, slimy, disgust-o worm slithering out of the small pile. Any minute it would touch Mrs. Iptweet's hand. I felt sick in my stomach.

I wanted to run and shiver, and maybe throw up, but I could see Mrs. Iptweet needed my help. No one else was around.

"Watch out, Mrs. Iptweet!" I shouted. "It's close to your bare skin. I'll go get a shovel and smash it, okay? Don't move. You don't want to get bitten by a wild worm."

Mrs. Iptweet laughed, "Zaady Gal, it's okay, worms don't bite. No need to smash this little guy."

The worm moved onto Mrs. Iptweet's bare, naked wrist. I felt faint.

"We've hit pay-dirt, Zaady Gal," Mrs. Iptweet said. "Worms in a garden are a very good sign."

"Really?" I gasped. "Do you think more than one slime-o worm lives in this dirt, Mrs. Iptweet?"

"Zaady Gal, we can only hope there are many, many worms in this dirt," said Mrs. Iptweet.

The thought of many, many worms made my knees feel all rubbery. I began to wobble.

"You look a bit pale, Miss Girl," she said. "I'll put this little fellow back in his rightful place so he can do his job. Let's you and I go inside and celebrate. Would you like some refreshment?"

I nodded.

"How about some juice and a crumpet?"

"Yes, please, Mrs. Iptweet," I said weakly. "What's a crumpet?"

"A crumpet is a yummy thing. The perfect antidote to Wild Worm Fear."

Mrs. Iptweet held my hand as we walked into the studio. She sat me down in her comfy chair with the blue stripes on it.

She said, "Focus on your breathing, Zaady Gal. Breathe slowly."

Mrs. Iptweet brought down a tray with two glasses, a pitcher, and crumpets on a plate. She handed me a glass full of juice. Then she held up her glass full of juice. We celebrated the Worm Sighting by drinking a toast.

"Chérie, worms mean the ground is alive and plants will

grow," said Mrs. Iptweet. "Let's drink to the Lively Living Earth."

We tapped our glasses together. I took a sip of juice. It tasted like cool pears. The crumpet was round like a cookie and puffy like a cake. I took a bite. It tasted like buttery bread. Yum. I could feel my strength returning.

Then I said, "Mrs. Iptweet, how come you're not grossed out by disgust-o worms?"

Mrs. Iptweet said, "Gradually, I've made friends with all parts of the Cycle of Life, Sheherazade, even the slithery, slimy-looking ones."

"I don't think I could ever touch a worm, Mrs. Iptweet."

"You don't have to, Sheherazade."

"Maybe I'm not cut out for Power-Tapping work, Mrs. Iptweet. It might be too slimy for me."

"I'll be so delighted if you continue, Zaady Gal. I think it's too soon to make a decision. Learning to Tap for Power takes time."

On my way home, I had a lot of thoughts and questions in my mind, like: how many wild worms are living in that dirt? Three? Fifty-seven? Two million? Does Mrs. Iptweet eat crumpets everyday? What will we do with all those piled-up stones?

That night, I wrote a letter to my Aunt Belle. I used my best ballpoint pen, the one with blue ink:

Dear Aunt Belle,

Do you like the smell of dirt? What is your opinion about worms? Did you ever eat a crumpet? I collect rocks now. You will get a surprise on your next visit to our house. The surprise will be in my room. If you need any help with your dreams, don't worry.

Love from Your Niece, Me

CHAPTER FOUR

The Power of the Ground

Almost every day in April, I visited Mrs. Iptweet and we tapped the Power of the Ground. This means we did a lot of digging, planting, and watering. I saw a lot of worms. In one day I counted thirty-two. I didn't have to touch the worms in order to count them or to be grossed out by them.

For power-tapping, Mrs. Iptweet liked to wear her big red apron with pockets, and her flowery bird nest hat. I liked to wear my jeans, my pink shirt with the butterfly design, and my old green sweater.

One day, after the whole patch of dirt was dug up, turned over, raked smooth, and sprinkled with water from the hose, Mrs. Iptweet said, "Sheherazade, it is time to plant the seeds."

I said, "Okey dokey, Mrs. Iptweet."

Mrs. Iptweet handed me an old shoe box. The shoe box was

painted with green leafy shapes all over it, and onto the lid of the box was glued a bunch of silky flowers.

"Are you ready, Chérie?" asked Mrs. Iptweet.

"Yes, ma'am," I said.

"Okay. Close your eyes." I closed my eyes.

"Now reach into the shoe box, and feel around."

I put my hand inside the box. I felt a lot of small papery packages.

"Pick out a pack of seeds. Don't peek. Let's let the seeds surprise us."

I pulled out a papery pack of seeds. Big letters on the front spelled SUNFLOWER. On the back of the packet there was a lot of information about SUNFLOWER: how tall it will grow and how to plant the seeds. The instructions said we must plant the seeds one inch deep and nine to twelve inches apart in a straight row. I opened the packet and handed thirteen black and white stripey seeds to Mrs. Iptweet.

Mrs. Iptweet said, "Time to bless the seeds, Sheherazade, and ask them to grow."

I said, "Oh, okay, Mrs. Iptweet."

We blew our breath on them and said encouraging words to the seeds, like "Grow, grow, grow, you Lovely Seeds," and "You are going to be great plants!" and "Thank you in advance for existing, Seeds."

Then Mrs. Iptweet tossed the seeds into the air above the dirt, and let the seeds fall wherever they wanted to. Some were close together, some far apart. The seeds looked like a starburst or a constellation on the dark brown ground.

I showed Mrs. Iptweet the seed packet. I pointed to the planting directions.

"Um, Mrs. Iptweet, see here where it says nine to twelve inches apart?"

Mrs. Iptweet smiled.

"Oh, that is a nasty rumor, Chérie. Pay no attention to limited thinking. Plants love a party atmosphere."

I said, "Oh."

"Would you like to help me poke the seeds into the ground, Sheherazade?"

"Sure, Mrs. Iptweet," I said. I gently pushed the sunflower seeds into the dirt about one inch deep. "What do you mean about Limited Thinking, Mrs. Iptweet."

Mrs. Iptweet was poking seeds into the dirt, too.

She said, "Well, Zaady Gal, limited thinking is when a person forgets that all kinds of wonderful things are possible, even things that seem impossible."

I thought about that for a minute. An idea came into my mind.

I asked, "Like when my mom says we absolutely don't live in an earthquake zone, but maybe we do?"

Mrs. Iptweet looked at me.

"Well, sort of, Chérie."

Each afternoon at Mrs. Iptweet's garden, I closed my eyes, pulled out a tiny package, and let the seeds surprise us. Here is what we planted and why: Sunflower, for golden majesty and tallness. Marigold, for spicy smells. Cosmos, for wispy purpleness. Red Poppy, for great beauty. Morning Glory, for glory in the mornings. Lettuce, for lunch. Swiss Chard, for dinner. Pumpkin, for dessert.

Sometimes during the afternoon planting time, Mrs. Iptweet and I were quiet. That's when I watched birds fly around and heard a lot of twittering and chirping. I noticed the smells of the dirt and growing things, and how the sunlight looked on the weeds in the back alley.

Sometimes during the afternoon planting time, Mrs. Iptweet and I talked. I told Mrs. Iptweet about my boring school and my boring life. Mrs. Iptweet told me about mysterious mysteries.

For example, one afternoon when all the seeds were planted and I was watering the dirt, Mrs. Iptweet said, "Ah, Sheherazade, the great powerful mystery of water and sunlight and dirt." Her words came out like a sigh.

Mrs. Iptweet fluffed her hair, and turned her face up to the sky, and breathed in a lot of air.

"Plants simply cannot resist the glory of dirt, sunlight, and water, Sheherazade. Neither can people."

I never thought about the Glory of Dirt before.

"Such a wonder, the Power of the Ground," said Mrs. Iptweet.

"Yeah, Mrs. Iptweet," I said. I kept watering and smelling the good smells.

"You know, Chérie, you are becoming a Power-Tapper Extraordinaire."

"Do you really think so, Mrs. Iptweet?"

She said, "Soon a flowery hat will be in order, Chérie."

I smiled and felt a giggle begin inside me. Then I felt a piece of sadness. I remembered about the flowery hat in my closet.

"I already have a flowery hat, Mrs. Iptweet," I said.

Mrs. Iptweet said, "Do you, Chérie?"

"It was my Gran Modesta's."

"Oh?"

I said, "When my Gran got too sick to do her gardening last summer, she gave her sun hat to me. My mom says I can save it until I'm grown up."

"What a lovely thing to have your Gran's hat, Sheherazade. Is it a treasure for you?"

I said, "Yes." I felt some tears come into my eyes.

Mrs. Iptweet asked, "Were you close to your Gran Modesta, Chérie?"

"Yes, Mrs. Iptweet. Gran and I read a lot of stories together. We used to sit on the extremely special rag rug she made just for me," I said. A tear fell down off my cheek and landed on the driveway, but I couldn't stop remembering.

"Oh, how wonderful," said Mrs. Iptweet. "You've experienced a great love in your life already, Chérie. And you are only nine."

Mrs. Iptweet came over to me and put one hand on my shoulder and her other hand on my head. A stream of tears was falling down my face. I wiped my eyes on the sleeve of my green sweater.

"Actually, I'm nine-and-a-half, Mrs. Iptweet."

"Please accept my condolences, Chérie, about the passing of your Gran." Mrs. Iptweet crouched down and hugged me.

I nodded my head and the tears kept on falling out of my eyes. My nose was full of snot from crying. It was hard to breathe with that much snot in my head. Mrs. Iptweet noticed I was gagging. She pulled a hankie out of her apron pocket and handed it to me. Mrs. Iptweet's hankie had pictures of tiny pink frogs all over it.

I gasped, "Thank you, Mrs. Iptweet," and blew my nose into the fancy froggy hankie.

Then I said, "Sorry to mess up your hankie, Mrs. Iptweet."

Mrs. Iptweet said, "Tears and weepy goop are what a hankie is for, Chérie. Don't worry, it all washes out."

"I don't like crying very much, Mrs. Iptweet."

Mrs. Iptweet wiped around my eyes. "Chérie, it's a great gift to cry for someone you love," she said. "Crying is an important part of the flow of life, Chérie."

I blew my nose again onto a pink frog.

"Let it out, Lovey Girl. Holding in sadness makes the sadness bigger." Mrs. Iptweet squeezed my hands and said that was enough gardening for today.

Upstairs in the kitchen, I sat at Mrs. Iptweet's bright blue kitchen table. Her kitchen now has pink walls. I guessed that Mrs. Iptweet's Redecoration Engineers had been at work.

Mrs. Iptweet used a clean washcloth to wipe off my face again. Then Mrs. Iptweet gave me hot lemony tea and pieces of apple with cinnamon sprinkled on top. My tears were all done, and I felt better.

Mrs. Iptweet said, "Shall I show you what is new around here, Chérie? You will be surprised, I think."

Mrs. Iptweet took my hand and led me all around her house to see the new colors on the walls: pink in the kitchen, yellow in the living room, aqua blue on the stairwell walls and bright green in the closet. Flower colors. I thought, Mrs. Iptweet's house looks like flowers having a party.

Mrs. Iptweet said, "Oliver and Phineas will be over next week to paint the trim all around." Ah ha, I thought, Mrs. Iptweet's grown-up sons are her Redecoration Engineers.

"I'm thinking a lovely lavender color would look nice. What do you think, Chérie?" Mrs. Iptweet asked.

I said, "Lavender is a great color, Mrs. Iptweet. I think lavender will look beautiful."

Then I said, "Bye for now, Mrs. Iptweet," and "Thank you for the refreshment, Mrs. Iptweet."

I walked home. I had red eyes, a dry nose and a spicy apple taste in my mouth.

That night, I couldn't sleep. I was awake in my bed underneath my bumpy pink bedspread for a long time. Finally, I sat up and turned on the little lamp on my bureau. I went into my closet and got out the big white hatbox. I opened the box and there it was: Gran's dark brown straw hat. It has a fluffy flower on one side. The color of the flower is lavender.

I lifted the big hat out of the box and put it on my head. It slipped down and covered my eyes completely. I could see myself in the mirror through the woven straw. Then I got a tee shirt out of my drawer and stuffed it in the hat and tried it on again. I only needed the one tee shirt and a pillowcase stuffed into the hat, and it fit me perfectly.

Last summer, Gran told me she had a feeling I would have a garden someday when I grow up. Gran said I could use her hat whenever I wanted to. That way I would remember her.

I said, "Thank you, Gran, I'll keep it forever."

I'm turning out to be a gardener sooner than we thought.

Gran's hat on me

CHAPTER FIVE

The Pyramid of Gravel

My Aunt Belle is a Professional Recycling Cowgirl Artist, and her hobby is sending oddball stuff through the U.S. mail. Aunt Belle likes to shake up the United States Post Office. She can't stand to think of mail-persons being bored with their very important jobs. Aunt Belle calls her unusual letters Postal Creations.

Addressed
baked bean can

Today after school, I found a Postal Creation from Aunt Belle in our mailbox. It was an addressed baked bean can. I could hardly wait to open it, but it was time to go over to Mrs. Iptweet's garden. I knew Mrs. Iptweet would like to see and learn about a Postal Creation.

I ran upstairs and put my book bag in my room. Right there on the floor I saw the big white box still open, full of Gran's hat. I sat for a minute and looked at her hat, and a nice feeling came into me, not sad.

I put on Gran's hat. I grabbed Aunt Belle's Postal Creation and walked carefully to Mrs. Iptweet's garden, balancing Gran's hat on my head.

Mrs. Iptweet saw me coming down the alleyway and waved. When I got close she said, "Your Gran's hat suits you very well, Sheherazade."

I showed Mrs. Iptweet the tee shirt and pillowcase stuffing.

Mrs. Iptweet said, "A brilliant solution, Zaady Gal, and congratulations on letting a treasure be part of your daily life."

I said, "Yeah, thanks, Mrs. Iptweet."

I showed Mrs. Iptweet my mail from Aunt Belle. Mrs. Iptweet turned the baked bean can over and over. We heard a rattling sound.

She said, "Chérie, your auntie wrote your address right on the can. And look, she taped the postage stamps right onto the can, too. Oh, the Amazingness of Life on earth."

I said, "Yes, Mrs. Iptweet, my Aunt Belle doesn't believe in regular envelopes."

"Oh my, this is fascinating, Sheherazade," Mrs. Iptweet said. "Is it time for you to open it?"

"Yes, I think it is time, Mrs. Iptweet."

I used Mrs. Iptweet's sharp knife to cut open the taped-up top. I reached inside the baked bean can and pulled out a blue plastic cowgirl figurine. Tied

Cowgirl figurine

onto the tiny plastic arm of the blue cowgirl was a folded-up note. I untied the secret note and opened it up. The note read:

Howdy, Sweet-Thing-Baby-Girl,

I'm thinking of you. We're doing a parade here for rodeo.

I'm gonna ride Bessie the Wonder Horse. Dress her up like a ballerina, just for fun. As you know, Bessie the Wonder Horse loves pink. Dirt smells fine to me and worms are honorable creatures. Thanks for asking. Here's a little something for your collection.

Love to you from Your Auntie Bellissima

Mrs. Iptweet laughed and laughed. She said, "That is so wonderful, Sheherazade. What an interesting letter your auntie wrote."

I said, "Yes, Mrs. Iptweet, it is so fun and exciting to get weird-o mail from my aunt."

Mrs. Iptweet still had some giggles giggling out of her.

"Once at Christmastime, my Aunt Belle sent me a big paper bag stuffed full of tinsel and a tiny note that said 'Dear Girl, Merry You-Know-What from You-Know-Who.' Aunt Belle wrote my address right on the big paper bag and used staples to close it, Mrs. Iptweet."

"What an unusual auntie!" said Mrs. Iptweet.

I said, "My mom thinks so, too, Mrs. Iptweet. When my Aunt Belle was born, her name was Edith. But then she grew up, and read an Italian novel, and became all inspired to be her true self. She changed her name to Bellissima, Aunt Belle for short."

"That is so interesting, Chérie," said Mrs. Iptweet.

"And once to celebrate Springtime, Aunt Belle sent me an egg carton tied together with pink string. It was full of plastic eggs with jelly beans and tiny chocolate eggs inside."

"Her correspondence is very creative, Chérie."

"Aunt Belle calls them her Postal Creations. She is an artist like you are, Mrs. Iptweet."

I read Aunt Belle's note again.

I said, "My Aunt Belle is so lucky to be in a parade, Mrs. Iptweet."

"Yes, parades are very wonderful, Chérie," said Mrs. Iptweet.

"I've never been to a parade, Mrs. Iptweet."

"Really, Chérie? Never?"

I shook my head. I asked, "Have you ever been to a parade, Mrs. Iptweet?"

Mrs. Iptweet hesitated for a minute. She shifted her feet around.

"Well, yes, I have been to a parade, Chérie. Many times, in fact."

I looked up at Mrs. Iptweet. "How many times, Mrs. Iptweet? How many parades?"

Mrs. Iptweet scratched her head. "Hmmm, I lost count a while ago, Chérie," said Mrs. Iptweet. "I've been to a lot of parades because I am a Parade Specialist, Chérie. I went to school and studied about Parades and Processions."

My eyes blinked. "Um, Mrs. Iptweet, you studied parades in school?" I asked.

I wondered what kind of a great school that must be.

"Yes, Chérie. In college. And as part of my studies, I've traveled the world to observe parades."

My eyes opened wide and my mouth dropped open like they usually do when I am surprised or shocked about something.

"All over the world, Mrs. Iptweet?"

"Yes, Chérie," said Mrs. Iptweet. "These days, I still go to parades because, well, because I love parades. Sometimes I give speeches about parades and world celebrations at colleges and universities."

"I didn't know a person could have a career of going to parades, Mrs. Iptweet."

"Life is amazing," said Mrs. Iptweet. "Prepare yourself to be amazed by the Amazingness of Life, Chérie."

Mrs. Iptweet nodded her head and smiled at me.

"Life is full of reasons to celebrate. I'm sure one day you will experience a parade, too, Chérie."

Mrs. Iptweet looked into the baked bean can again.

"Is there more, Chérie?"

I peeked into the Postal Creation. Yep. At the bottom of the can I saw a round bundle of blue tissue paper. I pulled out the bundle and unwound the tissue wrapping. Deep inside all the soft paper was a rock.

The rock was smooth dark gray with scaly white stuff sticking out of it. It fit right into my hand. Mrs. Iptweet and I looked at it closely. I turned it over and over. I couldn't believe what I was seeing.

"Mrs. Iptweet," I said. "It looks like seashells are in this rock."

Mrs. Iptweet put on her glasses and looked at the rock very closely, too.

She said, "Oh my, Chérie, you are right. This is an ancient rock. It's full of fossilized sea creatures. What a treasure!"

Now I had one treasure on my head and one treasure in my hand. I was glad to have a special rock from Aunt Belle to add to my collection of Dream-o-rama rocks. I put the ancient seashell rock into my jeans pocket.

Then Mrs. Iptweet made an announcement, "Sheherazade,

everything that needed planting is planted. Everything that needed watering is watered. Today is the day we turn our attention to the Pyramid of Gravel."

We stood beside the pile of stones, all the stones we had scooped up off the patch of dirt.

"What do we do, Mrs. Iptweet, to clean up this mess of stones?" I asked. "Do you have any trash bags?"

"No trash bags, Zaady Gal," Mrs. Iptweet said.

Mrs. Iptweet squatted down beside the pile of stones and picked up a handful.

She said, "This gravel was once magnificent rocks in the earth, Chérie, all breathing quietly, steady and strong."

"Huh? Breathing rocks?" I asked. "That's pretty funny, Mrs. Iptweet."

I smiled at Mrs. Iptweet. Mrs. Iptweet looked at me.

"Oh yes, Chérie, rocks are creatures in their own unique way. In olden times, some peoples called them the Rock Nation."

I said, "I really like rocks, Mrs. Iptweet, but I think you are kidding me about rocks being alive. Right?"

"I would never kid you about something as important as rocks, Chérie. Rock Beings have an essence, a quietness and a magic all their own."

I thought about the big creek rocks in my room. My own Rock Nation breathing in the dust bunnies under my bed.

Mrs. Iptweet held her hand over our pyramid of gravel.

She said, "We acknowledge the big beauty of these rocks, now made into much tininess. We now assist these stones in the reclaiming of their power."

I thought, maybe we will glue the pieces of gravel back together into their Big Rock Selves. It might take us a long time, but I don't mind at all.

I said, "I'll get your glue gun from the studio, Mrs. Iptweet."

Mrs. Iptweet's glue gun has a sparkly blue handle and extra sticky glue sticks, which have super strong holding power. This glue adheres to paper, glass, metal, plastic, china, wood, and probably even rock.

But that was not it, because Mrs. Iptweet said, "Thanks, Chérie, but no need to get the glue gun. We're going to work with what we've got here." Mrs. Iptweet kept on talking, "There's no turning back once a rock has been blasted to bits."

"No. No turning back," I said. I looked at the pile of stones. "If we aren't going to throw them in the trash, or glue them back together, then what are we going to do with them, Mrs. Iptweet?"

Mrs. Iptweet stood up and walked around the pile of tiny stones. Mrs. Iptweet scratched her head. "Well, I'm not exactly sure yet, Chérie."

Mrs. Iptweet rolled around the little pieces of rock in her hand.

She said, "Chérie, it's time to tune in to our Artist Minds."

I stood there for a second. My eyes and cheeks scrunched up because I had some confusion in my head.

"Okay, Mrs. Iptweet. I've never heard of that show before, Mrs. Iptweet. What station is it on? What time does the Our Artist Minds Show start, Mrs. Iptweet? Is it on radio or TV?"

Mrs. Iptweet cocked her head and looked at me with a puzzley look. Then she laughed out loud.

She said, "Oh, Sheherazade! Let me explain. Artist Mind is not a show at all. Although, that is not a bad idea."

I said, "Oh."

Mrs. Iptweet put her finger onto her lips.

"Let's see. Artist Mind. Artist Mind is a place inside each of us. Our Artist Mind is the mysterious part of us where Inspiration lives," said Mrs. Iptweet.

My face stayed scrunched up.

"It's the place where wonderful ideas come from, Chérie."

My eyes opened up a little. I thought about how I get good ideas sometimes. I thought they came from Out of the Blue.

Mrs. Iptweet said, "Artist Mind is the part in all of us that knows exactly what to do with blasted bits of rocks."

I said, "Oh."

"Let's be quiet for a moment, Chérie, and see what ideas come into our minds. Perhaps we will get an Inspiration."

Mrs. Iptweet and I were quiet for a while, even though being quiet is not my style. We puttered around and touched the stones and looked at the dirt and smelled the air and heard bird and car sounds. All of a sudden Mrs. Iptweet's eyes got wider, and she said, "Oh!"

I thought maybe an idea from Mrs. Iptweet's Artist Mind came into her regular mind and surprised her. Mrs. Iptweet put her hands on her hips.

She said, "Chérie, I have an idea."

I said, "I thought so, Mrs. Iptweet. I noticed when it popped into your mind."

"That was very observant of you, Chérie."

Mrs. Iptweet fluffed her hair.

"Chérie, I think we should make an Earth Art Creation."

"Okey dokey, Mrs. Iptweet. No problem. But what is an Earth Art Creation?"

"Watch closely, Sheherazade. See what you think."

Mrs. Iptweet began to arrange the small gravel pieces into a long curvy line. After a while I could see the shape of a spiral, like a faraway galaxy right on the cement driveway next to the garden.

"Chérie, a spiral is the symbol of the eternal flow of life," said Mrs. Iptweet. "It's a good shape to make next to a garden, don't you think?"

I said, "Yes, ma'am."

I put the stones in place at the center of the spiral because my feet are smaller.

"Chérie, you are standing in the swirling energy at the center of the universe. How does it feel?"

I did notice a swirly feeling in my toes. I said, "It feels pretty swirly, Mrs. Iptweet, but don't worry, I can handle it."

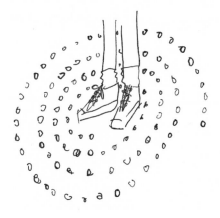

A swirly feeling in my toes

CHAPTER SIX

My Dream-o-rama

That night I was quiet during dinner with my mom. I kept having thoughts about rocks. The Rock Nation. The breath of rocks. I decided tonight is the night I will make my dreaming bed, my Dream-o-rama.

My mom was quiet at dinner, too. I knew she was stressed-out because her lips were in a straight line.

After a while my mom asked me, "What's going on in that head of yours, Girl?"

I didn't think my mom would understand about the Rock Nation under my bed so I said, "Nothing much, Mom. How was your day?"

She made a small smile and said, "Oh, fine I guess. That awful Mister Lunney made a math error today. It took me forever to straighten it out."

I said, "Oh, that's too bad, Mom. You have a pretty hard job don't you, Mom?"

My mom rolled her eyes, nodded her head, and ate another bite of Turkey Burger Surprise.

I was feeling all inspired to make my Dream-o-rama so I said, "You know, Mom, I'm really sleepy tonight. I think I'll go up to bed now."

My mom looked at me kind of funny and said, "Are you sick?" and felt my forehead.

I said, "No, Mom, I'm fine. Just tired." I rubbed my eyes. I yawned. "Goodnight, Mom. See you in the morning. You don't have to come up to tuck me in later. You just rest. Okay, Mom?"

My mom looked at me funny again.

"Okay, Darling Girl, good night and sweet dreams."

She kissed me on the cheek. I walked slowly up the stairs, then made a dash for my bedroom. I shut my bedroom door tight.

I dragged the heavy creek rocks out from under my bed. One by one, I put them on my bed in a circle. When they were perfectly arranged, I reached into my pocket and added the small ancient sea creature fossil rock from Aunt Belle. I put it at the top so my head will be near it. Then I climbed into the circle of rocks with my pillow and blanket. My bed was sagging from the heavy rocks but it felt really comfy in my Dream-o-rama. I smelled the smell of rocks. I could hardly wait to start dreaming, but first I wrote a letter to Aunt Belle:

Dear Aunt Belle,
I have added the great seashell fossil rock to my collection. Tonight I am going to have exciting dreams. Did you know that rocks breathe? Verrry slooowly.
Love from You Know Who

The Rock Nation under my bed

I woke up the next day but I had no dreams. Then I heard my mom coming up the stairs to wake me up. Uh oh, I thought. I jumped out of bed, threw my bedspread over the Dream-o-rama and ran to my bedroom door to meet Mom.

"Oh, hi, Mom, good morning. How are you today, Mom?" I asked.

"Oh, just fine, Darling Girl. How are you?"

She kissed me, but I could see her eyes looking into my room.

"Well, I'm up, Mom. I guess I'll get dressed now," I said. "See you downstairs, Mom. I'll just be a minute, Mom." I tried to close the door, but my mom put her foot next to it.

She said, "What are all those lumps on your bed, Kiddo?"

"Lumps? Oh, nothing, Mom."

My mom pushed past me, went right up to my bed and pulled back my pink bedspread. She looked at the rocks, then she looked at me.

Binky the rock

"Okay. I give up. Why are these rocks in your bed?" she asked.

I talked fast. "I want to have interesting dreams, Mom. Mom, I was going to make a tree bed, but I didn't want bugs to crawl on me so I decided to make a rock bed instead. Mom, did you know that rocks breathe? They're clean rocks, Mom. I washed them off, Mom."

My mom's eyes got big.

"In the sink?" she asked. I nodded. My mom put her hand onto her forehead.

She said, "Did you say something about breathing rocks? No, don't tell me. I don't want to know."

Aunt Belle says my mom is the rock in our family. But my mom does not look like a rock or a craggy mountain. She has a soft face, and big brown eyes, and short brown hair. She makes her hair curly by setting it every night in pin curls with about a hundred bobby pins. She likes to wear clothes that are tan or blue. My mom says she doesn't mind being the sensible one in a family full of nuts. She says, "Someone has to hold it all together."

My mom said, "Well, making maps and sleeping with rocks in your bed definitely smacks of our family's nutty streak. I was really hoping you'd be more like me, but it doesn't look too likely at this point, I guess."

I didn't say anything. My mom shook her head and went downstairs.

"I'll be right down, Mom," I said. "Don't worry, Mom. They're clean rocks. Honest, Mom."

For two weeks I slept in the middle of my Dream-o-rama nest, but I had no dreams. I tried everything to make it work. One night I talked to my rocks. Another night I gave them each a name: Pinky, Shiny, Blacko, Bozo, Speckles, Sparkles, Greeny Green, Banjo, Night Sky, Bumpy, Lumpy, Rocky and Binky. One night I pretended my finger was a lightning bolt, electronically charging each of my rocks with super-duper dreaming power. Still no dreams. Maybe these rocks are all worn out, I thought, maybe they are not real dreaming rocks.

Maybe my Dream-o-rama is a failure and I'll never be able to have interesting dreams.

That afternoon, I went to see Mrs. Iptweet. She was in her garage studio gluing sequins onto her sneakers. I told her all about my dream trouble.

Mrs. Iptweet said, "First of all, great idea to make a Dream-o-rama, Zaady Gal."

"Thanks, Mrs. Iptweet," I said.

"Second of all, Zaady Gal, you are having dreams each night, everyone does. You just aren't remembering them."

"Oh," I said.

"Have you asked your Awake Self to allow your dreams to be remembered yet?"

"No, Mrs. Iptweet. I haven't said anything to my Awake Self yet. But I did name the rocks."

Mrs. Iptweet put down her glue gun.

"That's great, Chérie. So few people ever take the time to name their rocks."

"Yeah," I said.

Mrs. Iptweet said, "Here's what I suggest, Chérie. Before you go to sleep, say these magic words: Dreams, dreams, I know you are here. Come into my mind, I have no fear."

I picked up Mrs. Iptweet's green sparkle pen and wrote down the magic words for dreaming.

"Thank you, Mrs. Iptweet," I said. "I never knew any real Magic Words before."

Mrs. Iptweet picked up her glue gun and added a few more red sequins to the toe of her sneaker.

"Your dreams can hardly wait for you to remember them, Chérie, so don't give up."

Then Mrs. Iptweet looked up and said, "It's a Tuesday today, isn't it, Zaady Gal?"

Tuesday is always the day when we change the Earth Art Creation into its next manifestation. This means we make a new design.

I said, "Yes, it is definitely a Tuesday today, Mrs. Iptweet."

Mrs. Iptweet said, "Well, what image shall we make today?"

So far, we had made a Spiral and a Dove of Peace design on the driveway with the gravel. Mrs. Iptweet tuned into her Artist Mind, which is pretty big and full of inspirations. Mrs. Iptweet got an inspiration right away.

She said, "Let's celebrate the glory of roundness this week, Chérie, and make a beautiful circle. Our sun, our moon and our very own planet Earth are all magnificently round."

Mrs. Iptweet picked up her sneakers.

"And so are sequins," she smiled.

"Good idea, Mrs. Iptweet," I said.

We gently swept aside the Dove of Peace and I began to make the circle shape. I know all the small stones really well now. Some of the stones have tiny ferns imprinted in them, some are full of sparkles. When we were done, Mrs. Iptweet and I stood there and admired the newest Earth Art Creation.

Then Mrs. Iptweet said, "Chérie, next Tuesday it will be your turn to choose an image for the Earth Art Creation."

I looked up at Mrs. Iptweet. I gulped and said, "Oh. Okay, Mrs. Iptweet."

Inside my mind though, I thought uh-oh, yikes, and oh, no.

I felt a lot of nervousness all week long. On Wednesday, I bit my nails. On Thursday, I ate a ton of chocolate and popcorn. On Friday, I kept bumping into things. On Saturday, I could not eat a thing. On Sunday night, I could not sleep.

On Monday, I went to Mrs. Iptweet's garden after school. Mrs. Iptweet was looking up at the clouds in the sky when I got there.

"Observing the heavens," she said, even before I asked.

I explained to Mrs. Iptweet that I didn't have even one interesting idea for an Earth Art Creation during the whole week.

"Probably some people don't have Artist Minds, Mrs. Iptweet," I said.

Mrs. Iptweet said, "Oh, Zaady Gal, that's a nasty rumor. Everyone has a large, expansive creative Artist Mind whether they know it or not."

"Then maybe mine is stuck or clogged up or something, Mrs. Iptweet, because I do not know what design to make for an Earth Art Creation tomorrow."

Mrs. Iptweet stood up, and turned to me.

"Well then, that is a problem. But all problems have solutions, Zaady Gal. Let's unstick that big expansive Artist Mind of yours, shall we?" said Mrs. Iptweet.

"Sure, Mrs. Iptweet," I said. "But what do we do?"

"First, take some nice deep breaths right into your belly, Chérie."

I breathed in and watched my stomach pouf out pretty far.

"Good job, Chérie. Now, please close your eyes."

I closed my eyes.

"No peeking," said Mrs. Iptweet. "We are going to contact your Artist Mind, Chérie. And Artist Minds like quiet and they like a lot of air."

The whole world was dark to me, and my belly was full of breath. Mrs. Iptweet leaned over close to my ear. I could smell the smell of Mrs. Iptweet. She smelled like seeds and air, and clean dirt and lemony shampoo.

Mrs. Iptweet whispered into my ear, "Hello, Chérie's Artist Mind? Are you in there? We know you are. How are you?"

I giggled.

"Well, hey there. Chérie is wanting to know you. We kindly ask you for an Inspiration for Chérie."

Mrs. Iptweet said to me, "Chérie, do you think your Artist Mind heard me all right?"

I kept my eyes closed and nodded my head up and down.

Then Mrs. Iptweet leaned in close to my ear again and said in her whispery voice, "Thank you so much, Chérie's Artist Mind. Chérie promises to pay attention and will notice you when you show up. Thanks for listening."

Mrs. Iptweet straightened up.

"Okay, you can open your eyes now, Chérie."

I opened my eyes. Mrs. Iptweet started to water the garden. I stood there for a minute, but nothing happened.

I said, "Nothing seems to be happening, Mrs. Iptweet. I don't feel any different."

I checked inside my brain. "Yep, still no ideas about you-know-what, Mrs. Iptweet."

Mrs. Iptweet said, "Well, Zaady Gal, we have asked your Artist Mind for an Inspiration. That is the first step. But we are not in charge of when your Artist Mind will open up and send you an Inspiration. Your job now is to keep breathing normally and go enjoy the rest of the day."

Hmmm, I thought. Keep breathing and go play?

"But, Mrs. Iptweet...," I said.

"The Inspiration will come, Chérie, I promise." Mrs. Iptweet smiled at me and turned off the water. "I'll see you tomorrow when it's time to move the stones."

At home that night I pushed the peas around my plate, studied some math, and worked on my science paper about cardinals and blue jays. Cardinals are reddish and blue jays are bluish. To spice up my boring science paper, I made a map of the neighborhood and puts X's on the trees where I have seen these birds. I took a bath with the honeysuckle soap Gran Modesta gave me. I tried parting my hair on the other side. I kept breathing. I read two chapters of my library book, and fell asleep about nine o'clock p.m. Guess what? I had a dream.

In my dream I saw whirling pinwheels of ducks, and a girl making a cloud of cheese in her hands. A lot of stones were laying around on the ground. The dream stones were saying stuff over and over with their big slow stone voices, "The Glooooory of Diiiiiirt," and "Oh, the Amaaaaazingness of Liiii-iiife." And an old stone, the very First Stone on Earth said, "Doooon't beeeee foooooled by dead-loooooking diiiirrrrrrt." Then I woke up.

That afternoon, I ran, ran, ran over to see Mrs. Iptweet. My head was bursting full of my exciting dream. When I got there, Mrs. Iptweet was washing out her brushes.

I said, "Mrs. Iptweet, have I got a big news flash for you."

After I told Mrs. Iptweet about my amazing and interesting dream, Mrs. Iptweet said, "Chérie, that is a truly great dream. It shows that your Artist Mind is alive and well."

I said, "Do you think so, Mrs. Iptweet?"

Mrs. Iptweet said, "Oh yes. Chérie, absolutely. It also shows me that we've been barking up the wrong creative tree for you."

"Huh, Mrs. Iptweet?" I asked.

"The stones in your dream weren't making themselves into designs, Chérie. They were speaking! I'd say that your creative Artist Mind has a special love for words, Chérie, maybe even stories."

I thought about this for a minute. It was true I liked to make up stories with Gran Modesta. I like writing to my Aunt Belle. My Aunt Belle says she loves my letters. And on my maps, I like to write in the names of things.

I told Mrs. Iptweet my thoughts and said, "I think you are right, Mrs. Iptweet."

Mrs. Iptweet shook my hand up and down. She said, "Today, Chérie, you have met your destiny with Creativity. Congratulations."

I said, "Yeah. Thanks, Mrs. Iptweet."

"So, Chérie," she asked, "what Earth Art *message* shall we make today?"

I thought about my dream and all the stone voices and what they said. I thought some more, then I decided on my favorite dreamy stone message.

"Don't Be Fooled By Dead-Looking Dirt," I said. "That's the message for today, Mrs. Iptweet."

Mrs. Iptweet smiled and said, "Okey dokey, Zaady Gal."

It took us about one hour to arrange the gravel just so.

Mrs. Iptweet said, "I feel so honored, Chérie, to be here at the World Premiere of your Movable Mosaic of Messenger Stones."

My face was all smiley.

I said, "Thanks, Mrs. Iptweet."

CHAPTER SEVEN

Mrs. Iptweet Slaps Her Legs

I could tell something was weird the minute I walked through our door. My mom was not napping as usual. She was sitting on the tan chair twisting a piece of her hair. My mom twirls her hair around her pointing finger until the strand of hair is wound really tight and pulls her hair roots away from her scalp. I stood at the doorway and said, "Mom, stop doing that, or I'll have to deal with a mom who is divorced *and* bald."

My mom said, "I got a postcard from your dad today. He'll be in town next week and he wants to visit you on Wednesday. He'll take you to dinner, I suppose. Like usual."

I said, "Oh. Okay, Mom, thanks for telling me."

I gave my mom a hug, and put my book bag upstairs in my room. Then I headed right over to Mrs. Iptweet's garden. On the way there, my mind was all huge excitement. My legs jumped up and down doing a funny dance step while I walked.

I didn't know how I would be able to wait a whole week to see my dad.

I now have a job at Mrs. Iptweet's garden. My job title is Lovely Assistant Power-Tapper Extraordinaire. It is a job I love. Part of my job is to talk to the plants. I say encouraging words like "You are doing so great!" and "Way to go, Plants!" I also arrange the stones and gravel into the Earth Art Creations on the driveway. In return, Mrs. Iptweet teaches me all about art and art supplies. So far I have learned sequin art, glitter art and sparkle pen art.

When I got to the garden, I checked the dirt for signs of life. At first the dirt looked regular plain dark brown. But then my eyes could see tiny green fuzz growing all over the place. I moved my hand across the green fuzz. It felt soft and feathery. The seeds in Mrs. Iptweet's garden were sprouted! I ran to Mrs. Iptweet's garage studio. At the studio doorway I said what I always say when I am announcing an important news flash to Mrs. Iptweet. I used my loud voice to yell: "Hey, Mrs. Iptweet, guess what?"

Inside the studio, I saw Mrs. Iptweet leaning on her elbows on her art table looking at something. Her art table was covered with stacks and stacks of books. I saw that today Mrs. Iptweet was wearing a bright yellow dress and red shoes and lacy pink socks. Mrs. Iptweet turned around and smiled when she heard my announcement voice.

She said, "Good afternoon to you, Zaady Gal. You seem very excited. What is it, Miss Girl?"

"Yes, Mrs. Iptweet, I am so excited. It's green fuzzy sprouts have come up, Mrs. Iptweet. I knew you'd like to know right away, Mrs. Iptweet."

"Oh, my. One wonderfulness after another, Sheherazade," said Mrs. Iptweet.

Mrs. Iptweet came outside with me and we looked at the green fuzz coming up out of the Glory of Dirt. We greeted the newborn plants and vegetables with welcoming words, like: "Welcome to life on Earth, Leafy Ones," and "Hey, looking good, Planties." The new plants just stood there and listened.

After a while Mrs. Iptweet said, "I've been unpacking my books today, Chérie. There is something in the studio that might interest you."

We went inside and walked over to Mrs. Iptweet's art table. In the middle of all the stacks of books on the table was one very large book. It had a dark red cracked leather cover. It smelled just like my dad's motorcycle jacket. I put my hands on the book. The leather felt cool and smooth, except for the cracked places. The edges of the book were shiny gold and the name of the book was stamped onto the cover in craggy gold. I thought, this must be some kind of olden magic book from olden times. And I was right because then I read the title: "*A Treasure Trove of Imaginary Animals, The Creatures of Myth, Mystery, and Magic of Olden Times.*"

I said, "This is a mysterious-looking book, Mrs. Iptweet. I like mysterious stuff, Mrs. Iptweet."

Mrs. Iptweet nodded. "Yes, Zaady Gal, mysterious mysteries are crucial to our happy existences. Go ahead, Chérie, open it up."

I opened the book. It was full of fancy swirly writing and drawings of unusual animals. I saw drawings of dragons, and on other pages were drawings of unicorns. I sat and turned the pages one by one.

"The Mythical Creatures, Chérie. The pretend Beasts and Beauties born in the imaginations of human beings throughout all of time," said Mrs. Iptweet.

I came to a whole chapter about mermaids. There were

"Treasure Trove" book opened to the Dragon page

drawings of mermaids from the South Seas, and mermaids from the deep northern waters. All the mermaids had long beautiful hair that floated in the salty oceans. I thought about how I would like to grow my hair long, and let it float all around me in the bathtub.

Mrs. Iptweet said, "Many people don't understand about Mystery, Myth, or Magic, Chérie. It is so sad, I feel."

Mrs. Iptweet shook her head.

"It seems our culture suffers from an Overdose of Logic, Zaady Gal."

I said, "Yeah, Mrs. Iptweet. An Overdose of Logic. It's a real problem all right."

Mrs. Iptweet flopped her arms at her sides, and breathed a deep breath.

She said, "More magic, Chérie. I think the remedy might be more Magic and more Mystery."

"I think you are right about that, Mrs. Iptweet. But how?"

Mrs. Iptweet said, "Now that is an excellent question, Chérie."

I closed up the book and we went outside again to be near the growing garden. Mrs. Iptweet sat down in her red plaid aluminum folding chair and fluffed her red hair. Mrs. Iptweet didn't say anything for a while. I could tell Mrs. Iptweet was deep in her own thoughts, because she looked out in front of herself, not at anything in particular. I sat in the other aluminum folding chair, the pink and green plaid one, and looked at the newborn plants coming up out of the ground.

Mrs. Iptweet looked at me and took a deep breath. She said, "Chérie, I have an idea."

I looked at Mrs. Iptweet but I didn't say anything.

Then Mrs. Iptweet spoke, "I think we ought to have a parade."

My eyes bugged out of my head.

"Have a parade?" I asked.

Mrs. Iptweet nodded her head up and down. I thought Mrs. Iptweet has an interesting mind, full of surprises.

"Parades are good for the soul, Chérie. They have a lot of magic to them. In my opinion, the world cannot have too many parades, Sheherazade."

"No, I guess not, Mrs. Iptweet," I said.

"A parade would be a good way for me to meet more of my new neighbors," said Mrs. Iptweet.

"You mean we'll have a parade here on Durham Street, Mrs. Iptweet?"

"Yes, Chérie. All great parades begin at home."

"Oh, right," I said. "But, Mrs. Iptweet, where do we get a parade from?"

Mrs. Iptweet sat up straight in her chair and said, "Well, ..."

I interrupted Mrs. Iptweet, though, because I figured it out.

"Oh, I know, Mrs. Iptweet, I bet there is a catalog we could order a parade from. My mom says there's a catalog for everything, and it's so convenient and economical to shop by catalog."

"That is very true, Chérie. But no, not from a catalog do we get a parade," said Mrs. Iptweet. "We make a parade, Chérie."

"Oh," I said. "What do we make it out of, Mrs. Iptweet?"

"Out of a lot of people and a lot of heart," Mrs. Iptweet said.

I looked at Mrs. Iptweet. A lot of thoughts were swirling around in my head. Mrs. Iptweet stood up.

"There is an important day coming up, Chérie," said Mrs. Iptweet. "The Summer Solstice is right around the corner."

I looked at Mrs. Iptweet. I didn't say anything.

"It's the longest day of the year on our side of the earth," explained Mrs. Iptweet. "We will be saturated with sunlight that day, Chérie. A great day to parade around, don't you think?"

Mrs. Iptweet crouched down and let her hand brush over the feathery green growing fuzz.

I gulped and said, "I don't know, Mrs. Iptweet. Around here nowadays, Summer Solstice is not such a big deal. It's a small deal, you know?"

Mrs. Iptweet said, "Well, in olden times Summer Solstice was one of the biggest party celebrations of the year. It was the middle of the summer growing season, and they called it Midsummer's Day."

I said, "Oh. Midsummer's Day."

Mrs. Iptweet stood up and said, "The Summer Solstice is still listed on our calendars, Chérie. Deep down inside everyone, even today, we know it is a day worth noting."

Mrs. Iptweet started to pace.

"We'll need a theme, too, Chérie," she said. "Something that will inspire people to dress up. Something that will get their imaginations going. Something that will fill their hearts with so much heart they will have to celebrate on Midsummer's Day."

Mrs. Iptweet stopped pacing. She closed her eyes and let the warm sun shine on her face. She looked down at me.

"I guess the Power of the Sun could be a theme, Chérie. What do you think?"

"A Sunshine Parade, Mrs. Iptweet?" I asked. I didn't think that many people would be inspired by this idea.

I said, "Um, the sun comes up every day, Mrs. Iptweet. I think people are kind of used to it."

Mrs. Iptweet made the tsking sound and said, "You are probably right about that, Chérie. Well, let's ask our Artist Minds for more Inspiration."

Mrs. Iptweet scratched her head and put her hands on her hips.

I said, "Okay, Mrs. Iptweet."

I squeezed my eyes shut, and took a deep breath. I wondered how I would get an idea because what did I know about parades? I never saw a parade in my life. I have no experience at all with choosing a parade theme. After a minute of no ideas popping into my mind, I opened my eyes. I stood up and looked up and down the back alleyway. Mrs. Iptweet was looking at the new plants growing in the patch of dirt. I wandered back inside Mrs. Iptweet's studio and sat down in front of the big leather creature book. I paged through it for a while. My Gran Modesta would really like this book, I thought.

All of a sudden, an idea rushed into my brain. A big inspiration filled up my whole mind.

I used my loud voice to call Mrs. Iptweet, "Hey, Mrs. Iptweet, guess what! I have a big inspiration about a parade theme. A truly great parade theme, Mrs. Iptweet."

Mrs. Iptweet came into the studio.

"What is it, Miss Girl?"

I pointed at the giant golden book.

"Mythical Creatures, Mrs. Iptweet. How about we make it a

Mythical Creatures parade? Pretend animals are extremely interesting and inspiring, I think."

Mrs. Iptweet looked at the Treasure Trove book, and then at me. Her eyes got wide and sparkly.

She said, "Ah, yes. A celebration of the mysterious, mythical creatures who don't actually live in the World of Form."

I said, "Huh? Oh, yeah. Exactly, Mrs. Iptweet."

"It's a brilliant idea for our parade theme, Sheherazade."

"Thank you, Mrs. Iptweet."

Mrs. Ipweet moved her hand across the air like a banner.

"A Mythical Creatures Parade on Midsummer's Day! The ideal remedy for too much logic in the world, Sheherazade."

"I'm glad you like the idea, Mrs. Iptweet," I said.

"And an excellent way, Chérie, to bring mystery and magic to our neighborhood."

I said, "Yes, Mrs. Iptweet."

Then I had another thought. "Mrs. Iptweet," I said, "I think a Mythical Creatures parade on Durham Street is a good idea, but what if no one will do it."

Mrs. Iptweet opened her eyes wide and said, "Why do you think that, Miss Girl?"

I said, "Because nothing ever happens on this street, Mrs. Iptweet! Mrs. Romero's parakeet, Señora Puff o' Fluff, escaped last year, but only for five minutes. And the sidewalk cracks never get any bigger. And there are no Talking Pigs or Interesting Anythings. I think people like it to be boring around here."

Mrs. Iptweet looked at me. She rubbed her chin and tapped her cheek for a whole minute.

"Well then, we simply must do it, Sheherazade. It's our mythic duty to organize the Mythical Creatures Midsummer's Day Parade," said Mrs. Iptweet. "We cannot let people around here continue to suffer from lack of mystery and passion, Chérie."

Mrs. Iptweet slapped her hands onto her legs.

"We have chosen an important day and an inspiring theme. We cannot go wrong!"

Uh oh, I thought, there's no way out of it now. When Mrs. Iptweet slaps her legs, it's a done deal.

We got right to work planning the parade. Mrs. Iptweet brought crumpets and mint tea to the studio to help keep up our strength.

Mrs. Iptweet said, "Well, how shall we introduce our idea to the neighborhood, Chérie? What do you think?"

"Mrs. Iptweet," I said, "I think it's going to be a big job. Maybe we should use your bullhorn."

Mrs. Iptweet handed me a bluebird cup full of tea. I drank a sip and my whole head and neck filled up with a big mintyness.

"The bullhorn is an excellent idea, Sheherazade, loud and dramatic," said Mrs. Iptweet.

"Thanks, Mrs. Iptweet," I said. "Should I go get it now?"

"But the bullhorn, I find, is better for controlling crowds than for creating them, Chérie. Perhaps we will use the bullhorn on Parade Day itself."

I said, "Oh, right. Okay, Mrs. Iptweet."

"We might start with a sign or two announcing our idea," said Mrs. Iptweet.

I said, "A sign? You mean like a billboard? We don't have any big billboards on our street, Mrs. Iptweet. This is a residential area. But my dad is coming to visit me next week, Mrs. Iptweet. On Wednesday. On Wednesday, I could ask my dad to make us a billboard. He knows how to make stuff."

"A billboard is another good idea, Chérie."

I said, "My dad is extremely busy playing his banjo all over the country, Mrs. Iptweet, so I don't know for sure. I'll ask him when we are eating dinner. He is coming to see me on Wednesday to take me out to dinner. I don't know yet where we are going, but he knows a lot of good places to eat."

Mrs. Iptweet said, "How wonderful your dad is coming to visit you, Chérie. Your dad sounds like an interesting fellow."

"Oh, yes, Mrs. Iptweet, he is," I said.

Mrs. Iptweet asked me to be in charge of writing down the Parade Planning Ideas. Mrs. Iptweet handed me a tablet of yellow paper and a purple glitter pen. Purple glitter ink is a truly great ink for writing down anything. I wrote on my Parade List:

#1. Bullhorn for Crowd Control on Parade Day

#2. Billboard - ask Dad to build one

"I'm thinking, Chérie, that in the meantime, you and I could make some small signs and put them up where our neighbors can see them, Chérie."

"Okay, Mrs. Iptweet, that works for me."

I added to my list: #3. Make small signs

Because my Artist Mind likes words so much, Mrs. Iptweet put me in charge of all the words on the Parade Signs. Here is what I wrote:

Attention All Neighbors!
Guess what, this is your Lucky Day.
A Midsummer's Day Mythical Creatures Parade is going to happen soon on Durham Street.
You can be in it!
June 21st, the Longest Day of the Year.
Meet up early at the back alley.
SIGN UP NOW!
Leave us a note at Mrs. Iptweet's house, #406.
Sincerely, Your Friends,
The Official Parade Organizing Committee

Mrs. Iptweet says I have real talent when it comes to words, sentences, and sign-making. We decorated the paper signs with glitter pens, crayons, and rubberstamps. I used a mermaid stamp and a star stamp on the signs. We punched holes in the top of the heavy sign paper with Mrs. Iptweet's hole puncher. We used Mrs. Iptweet's favorite hot pink string to tie the signs onto the big maple trees on our street. Mrs. Iptweet tied the signs up high on the trees. I tied the signs low. Our neighbors are all different sizes. I taped some signs onto the sidewalk for the people who only look down when they walk. When Mrs. Iptweet saw the sidewalk signs, she smiled and laughed, then patted my head.

"Oh, Miss Girl, you think of everything!" she said. "Good job, Chérie."

I said, "Thanks, Mrs. Iptweet."

When we were done, we looked up and down the street at our first parade organizing work. The signs fluttered in the breeze and made flapping sounds.

Mrs. Iptweet said, "The trees are our messengers to the neighborhood, Chérie."

I said, "Yes, Mrs. Iptweet. The trees here are great."

Mrs. Iptweet said, "Now, Chérie, it's time for us to watch and wait for the parade to take form."

That night I got all cozy in my Dream-o-rama bed, said the magic words for dreaming, and wrote a note to my Aunt Belle:

Dear Aunt Belle,
    Guess what? I have met my Destiny with Creativity and my dad is taking me out to dinner next Wednesday and I am making a parade for Midsummer's Day with Mythical Creatures.
    How are you?

    Love, Your Niece

CHAPTER EIGHT

The Visit of Dad

"Your dad will be here in ten minutes. I'm going for a walk."
I said, "Okay, Mom. Have a nice walk, Mom."

My mom gave me a quick hug and went out the door. I took myself and my book bag upstairs to my room. I closed the door. My mind was all huge excitement.

"Oh, goody," I said to myself, "a motorcycle ride with my dad and anything I want for dinner!" My legs did a jumping spinning dance on my rag rug. My arms waved around, and my mouth said, "Yes, yes, super-duper yes-o-rama."

I wondered where we would go to dinner tonight. Last time, my dad took me to the best hot dog place in the whole city. He likes his hot dog smothered with the works. That means ketchup, sauerkraut, onions, green chile, and lemon pepper. I like mine with mustard and relish. We had large root beers, two extra bags of chips, and three brownies for dessert. One brownie for me, two for my dad. It was really fun and interesting.

My dad has been everywhere, including west of the Mississippi River. My dad always brings a helmet and his old leather bomber jacket for me to wear while riding on his motorcycle. The jacket comes down to my knees so I am mostly protected from getting windburn or scratched by branches when riding on his motorcycle. My mom makes him drive slowly with me on the

Postcard from Dad

bike, but once in a while on a clear stretch he goes a little faster. My dad doesn't want to make my mom mad. He says he is on thin ice with my mom.

I took off my blue tee shirt and put on my red and white striped blouse, with the butterfly design on one side. It is my dress-up-for-a-dad-visit shirt. I combed my brown hair and washed my pink face. I smoothed my green shorts, pulled up my yellow socks, and wiped some dirt off my white sneakers.

When I heard the roar of my dad's motorcycle coming up the street, I opened up my top bureau drawer and took out my three maps. Two are finished. I am still working on the third one. My dad has already seen the first one I made, but I will show him again so he can see I am getting better at making maps. I carefully put my maps on top of my bed. My dad will show great excitement when he sees my progress in the field of Budding Cartography.

I heard my dad's voice downstairs.

"Hey, Honeybun, are you in there? Knock, knock. I'm here. Where are you, Honeybun? It's me. Dad."

My dad calls me Honeybun because he thinks I am so sweet

and he likes sweetness. I ran down the steps and opened the door.

I said, "Hi, Dad, I was upstairs getting my maps out to show you. Sorry to keep you waiting, Dad. Do you want to see my maps, Dad? How are you, Dad?"

My dad came inside, crouched down, and gave me a big hug. My dad is as big as a bear. It felt really good

Butterfly design on my dress-up-for-dad shirt

to feel his big strength squeezing me tight. I kissed his scratchy cheek and breathed in his smell. My dad smells like a bear, too, furry and leathery. That's because he has a big mustache and long black hair, and he wears a leather jacket. I squeezed him as hard as I could, so he could feel my strength and how much I missed him, too.

My dad's real name is Andrew. My dad's grown-up friends call him Bear. Bear is his nickname. I would like to call him Bear, too, but my dad likes it better if I call him Dad. He kissed my cheek and said he was just great and I grew a foot and what a sweetie I am.

I said, "Do you want something to drink, Dad? We have milk or water, Dad. Do you want to use your favorite old glass with the handle on it? I keep it upstairs in my room, Dad. It's no trouble for me to go get it. My new map is up there. Would you like to come see my new map, Dad? Come on up and I'll show you."

My dad said, "Okay, Honeybun, let's go take a peek at your map. You're still into that, huh?"

"Dad," I said, "mapmaking is interesting to me. I think it's a good thing to get started young for a career in mapmaking, you know. You said I have talent in this area, Dad."

"Yeah, I guess I did say that. And it's true, Honeybun. Let's go see what you've got."

We walked up the stairs to my room. My dad has to bend his head down to get through the doorway. He sat on the floor. My rag rug disappeared under him.

"Here is my first map, Dad, of my bedroom," I said. I handed the map to him.

He nodded his head and said, "Oh, yeah, I remember. It's terrific, Honeybun."

I said, "This one is my second map, Dad. It's a map of our boring street. Notice how improved it is from my first map?"

He said, "Oh yeah, Honeybun. It is very improved. Wow."

He looked at it for a while. I pointed out all the best features.

He said, "I like how you marked the sidewalk cracks. You don't miss a thing, do you, Honeybun?"

I explained how I measure the cracks in the sidewalks each week. If there is any tectonic plate-shifting or earthquaking around here, I will be the first to know.

Then I showed him my newest map.

The Kitchen what-not drawer

"It's not completely done, Dad. I'm still working on it. It's a big project, Dad. It's taking me a long time. I thought I'd show it to you anyway, Dad, since you're here, okay? Do you like it?"

He took my map in his big hands and looked at it. After a minute he said, "I like it a lot, Honeybun. It's great. Very complicated. Uh, what is it exactly?"

I said, "Dad, it's a map of the inside of the kitchen what-not drawer, you silly! There is a lot of stuff in it. Look here. These are the rubber bands and this is a twist tie. Sometimes I have to erase and change it because Mom keeps moving things around. This is my most complicated map so far, Dad."

The mug of Dad

I pointed out the balls of old string, the scotch tape dispenser, a box of matches, my old barrette, six bobby pins, and the dull scissors on the map.

My dad admired my map awhile longer before he said, "Honeybun, this is pretty wild. You have a really interesting mind, Honeybun. I see greatness in your future."

I could tell my dad was proud of me.

"Thanks, Dad," I said.

I got his favorite glass from my bureau drawer. We went into the bathroom and filled the glass with water. He took a long drink.

Dad said, "Let's go, Honeybun, I'm starved. How about we do Italian this time?"

I said, "Oh, wow, Dad, that sounds great. I like Italian food a lot, Dad."

My dad suited me up in the helmet and the leather jacket and lifted me onto the motorcycle. I sit behind him on the seat. My arms are too short to reach all around my dad, the Bear, so I hold onto his belt loops, and lean against his back. Even though we are riding on a dangerous motorcycle, I feel safe and happy. It's really fun to ride on a motorcycle, especially if you like wind as much as I do. It is definitely not boring to ride on a motorcycle with your dad. I wish my dad lived near me. He could ride me to school everyday.

We went to Mama Mia's Meatball Palace, a great place to eat. We sat in a booth with red plastic cushiony seats. The tablecloth was red and white checked, just like in Italy, I bet. The good food smells made my mouth water. My dad said to order whatever I wanted. I told the waiter I'd like Lasagna, and Meatballs di Venice and Spaghetti, a large orange soda, and two pieces of Boston cream pie for dessert.

My dad said, "Way to go, Girl."

He ordered a steak for himself. Dad said he would help me finish off my food if I got too full.

I said, "Okay, Dad." My dad is very considerate that way.

While we waited for the dinner food to get ready, I gave my dad my report about me and my school: I'm fine. My teacher is fine. My grades are fine. School is boring, but fine.

I asked my dad where he has been, and what banjo gigs did he play.

My dad said, "Oh, I've been around, out and about. Did a fun gig in Chattanooga. It was the wedding of an eighty-year-old woman to a seventy-seven-year-old man. They could still dance a polka, I just had to slow it down a bit for them."

I said, "Wow, Dad. You have an exciting life, Dad."

My dad told me about his other gigs in the South, too, and about how it's pretty tough to ride a motorcycle through the southern states. There are so many flying insects everywhere. He has to wear his visor down all the time and wipes it frequently.

I thought about the squished dead bugs on my dad's helmet.

I said, "Eeew, Dad, that's really interesting but it's disgust-o, too."

The waiter brought us our plates of food.

"Yeah, I guess so, Honeybun. Sorry. Hey, let's eat."

My dad took a bite of his steak. I ate a mouthful of meatball. A drip of red sauce dripped onto my shirt. Darn. But it blended in pretty good with the red stripe. We were quiet. We ate and ate for a while.

After eating my second meatball, I decided to tell my dad the big news and ask him the big question I had for him.

"Dad, guess what, something huge is going to happen on Durham Street. Something really gigantic and big."

He said, "Honeybun, it's really hard to predict an earthquake, don't get your hopes up, because..."

"Dad," I said, interrupting, "we're having a parade. A parade is going to happen on our very own street, Dad. I'm helping to organize the parade and everything. We have an important day and an inspiring theme, Dad."

"No kidding?" my dad said. "That's great, Kid."

"Yes, Dad, no kidding. It's the Midsummer's Day Mythical Creatures Parade, Dad. Midsummer's Day is an ancient partying holiday from olden times, Dad."

My dad kept on nodding and eating his steak and my spaghetti.

I said, "Dad, are you listening? This is really important and amazing."

"Yes," Dad said, "I'm all ears, Honeybun."

"My friend, Mrs. Iptweet, is a really interesting person, Dad. I'm her Lovely Assistant. We are working on the parade, and other projects, too."

"That's great, Honeybun," my dad said. "Can I have that meatball?"

"Sure, Dad." I used my fork to plop the meatball onto my dad's plate. "I'm learning about Tapping the Power of the Ground, too, Dad. That's means gardening, Dad."

I ate a big bite of lasagna.

"Gardening is good, Honeybun. Your Gran Modesta was a great gardener," Dad said.

Then he said, "How's your mom doing these days?"

He took a drink of water. I finished chewing the last meatball. I was full of Meatballs di Venice.

I said, "She still gets sad sometimes."

"I bet she misses Modesta something crazy. They were close, those two," my dad said. "It's a time thing, Honeybun. Your mom is getting used to life without Modesta. You hang in there, Honeybun, it'll get better."

"Yeah," I said.

Dad took a big gooey bite of the lasagna.

"I guess it's like when I had to get used to my life without you, Dad."

My dad coughed. He choked a little bit and spit out a cheesy glob. He looked at me, all flustered.

"Well jeez, Honeybun, it's not like I'm dead is it? I mean, here I am and all."

He wiped the goo out of his mustache and put his napkin on the table.

"Oh, no, Dad, you're not exactly dead completely. It's like you die, then you come back to life again for a nice dinner. It's definitely not like you are totally dead or anything. It's great, Dad. I'm used to it now, Dad, really," I insisted.

My dad's pie

The waiter took our plates away and brought the cream pies and a coffee for my dad. My dad looked at the pie but did not pick up his fork. When my dad looks at pie, but does not eat it right away, it means he is feeling upset. I changed the subject.

"Dad, I have something really important to ask you, Dad. We need somebody to build a billboard on our street. To tell about the parade. I know you are busy, but Dad, could you build us one tomorrow? Or tonight? We only need it to be about six or seven feet high."

My dad rubbed his face really hard with both his hands. Then he said, "Honeybun, I'd like to help you out. But it's been a while since I did any construction. And I sold my tools, and besides, I'm heading out to do a wedding tomorrow. So I…."

I said, "Oh. That's okay, Dad."

My dad poked his fork into his cream pie and smeared it around his plate. His face was frowny. I could tell he felt bad about selling his tools and everything. I don't like to see my dad all sad. I like it better when my dad eats his pie.

We were quiet for a little while. I took a bite of my creamy pie. I looked around the room and an idea popped into my mind.

I said, "Hey, Dad, I have an idea. It came into my mind just this minute, Dad."

My dad looked up at me.

"Um, maybe you'd like to play banjo for the Midsummer's Day Parade, Dad?" I said. "I know it's small potatoes for you Dad, but…"

Then another idea came into my mind, a truly great idea.

"You could be a Mythic Animal, Dad," I added. "Maybe a ferocious Mythic Bear! You could scare everyone. You're naturally big and ferocious-looking, Dad, especially when you don't comb your hair. It's a great idea, Dad! You could be the Stupendous and Terrifying Banjo-playing Bear from Ancient History, Dad! What do you think, Dad? I think it's great, Dad."

My dad put his head in his hands. He took a big deep breath and let it out.

"Well, that's not a bad offer, I guess. Not bad at all for a scary-looking dead dad," he said. "Would it help if I called you on the phone sometimes? Would I seem less dead to you, Honeybun?"

I said, "Calling is good, Dad."

He said, "I'll see what I can do, Honeybun, about the parade. When is it, again?"

I told my dad the details about when and where. My dad ate his pie and I finished mine. Then my dad paid the bill and left a tip. My dad was in a thoughtful mood. I kept quiet and we headed out to the bike. When we got to the motorcycle, my dad put the helmet on me and then the leather jacket. He started to zip up the big jacket zipper.

My dad asked me, "Do I scare you, Honeybun? I mean, am I a big scary bear to you?" This made a giggle gurgle out of me.

I said, "No way, Dad. To me, Dad, you are a big teddy bear."

He smiled and finished zipping up my jacket.

He said, "Honeybun, you are something else."

He kissed my cheek, swung me onto the bike, and we headed home.

Dad stopped the bike in front of our house, lifted me up off his bike and held me. I put my arms around his neck. My feet dangled in the air. It feels really cool to be up that high. Maybe I will grow up to be as tall as my dad. I am tall for my age.

It also feels really sad to me up there, because I know my dad is leaving again. I felt my chest get tight, and some burning tears came into my eyes.

He said, "Thanks for coming out with me, Honeybun. You're my girl, you know."

"Yeah, I know, Dad. Thanks for the great dinner, Dad." A little sob came out of me.

My dad said he wouldn't come in, and I should keep the helmet and jacket for our next visit. He hugged me tight and kissed both my cheeks. He smelled like Italian spices. I hugged him and kissed one of his rough cheeks.

My dad set me down. He took an envelope out of his pocket and gave it to me.

"This is for your mom," he said.

He tucked the envelope into my jacket pocket.

"And this is for you."

My dad put a twenty-dollar bill in my other pocket. He said to use it for something fun.

"I'm sorry I can't make the billboard for you, Honeybun. And I don't know for sure yet about the parade thing, but I'll do what I can. Okay, Honeybun? You go on in now."

"Okay, Dad. Bye, Dad," I said. My tears made my eyes all blurry.

"And I'll see about getting one of those cell phone things, okay?"

"Yeah, okay, Dad," I said.

"I love you, Honeybun," said Dad.

"I love you too, Dad."

I threw him a kiss. I stumbled up the steps to our porch.

My dad always waits until I am inside the house before he rides away. He wants to know I am safely home, that I am not abducted by any criminals that might be lurking around on our street. I got to the porch and turned around to wave goodbye to my dad. He gave me his goodbye. He holds his arm up high and moves his hand in a gentle wave. I waved too, and went inside.

I heard the noisy sound of him riding away on his motorcycle. My tears spilled onto my cheeks. What a mess. I wiped my face on the leather jacket sleeve. The wetness left a mark on the faded leather.

My mom was in the kitchen. I peeked into the envelope my dad tucked into my pocket. It was full of money and a note my eyes were too blurry to read. I took it in to my mom.

My mom put her ams around me and then used her blue dish towel to wipe away my tears.

"Always the same," she said, shaking her head.

I said, "I feel like going to bed, Mom. Okay? We had a great dinner. I ate a lot of meatballs and cream pie. I'm tired."

I gave my mom a kiss and went to my room.

I found a special place on my closet floor for Dad's jacket and helmet. I put the money he gave me in my underwear drawer with the other money he gave me. I'm saving up for a motorcycle. I climbed into the circle of rocks on my bed, my Dream-o-rama, and got all cozy. I fell asleep feeling sad and happy at the same time.

CHAPTER NINE

A Lot of Stuff Happens

Our parade signs flapped in the breezes for one whole week. But even with all that flapping, not one single person signed up to be in our parade. Mrs. Iptweet and I had a special Emergency Meeting of the Parade Organizing Committee. During our Emergency Meeting, Mrs. Iptweet and I had a serious discussion about our parade disaster. We also ate mango jam on crackers and sipped coconut milk, just like Mythic Mermaids from the South Seas.

I said, "I think our parade idea is not going to work, Mrs. Iptweet."

"Things do look a little grim, don't they, Chérie."

"Mrs. Iptweet, if no one does it, our parade will be a failure."

I sipped a sip of the sweet, tropical milk.

"A nasty rumor, Chérie!" she said, "No such thing as a failure. This is what we call a Learning Experience."

Mrs. Iptweet spread some jam onto her fancy cracker.

"It's not time to give up on our parade yet, Chérie," said Mrs. Iptweet. She patted my leg. "Let's go water the garden and ask for an Inspiration about what to do next."

We wiped our mouths with Mrs. Iptweet's orange napkins and headed out to the garden.

Lettuce and jam

It was a bright sunny day. It felt good to be outside and smell the smell of June. Sweet, and flowery, and grassy. It's the smell that happens right before school lets out for the summer, so it is a smell I love. Mrs. Iptweet and I stood there on the driveway feeling the warm sunshine on our skin. I turned on the water and held the hose; Mrs. Iptweet held her chin. I looked at the plants; Mrs. Iptweet observed the heavens. We both took lots of nice deep breaths and inside our minds asked for Inspirations about our Midsummer's Day Mythical Creatures Parade.

The plants were doing great, and I told them so. The lettuce was big enough to pick, so I picked some and put the leaves in my pocket.

Mrs. Iptweet said, "Chérie, I think it is clear that to bring our parade into the World of Form, we must take another action."

I noticed the pumpkin vine was getting long, and curly threads were reaching out. I put tiny sticks along its path so the vine could hold onto something as it grows.

I said, "I think you are right about that, Mrs. Iptweet. But what action?"

"That is the question, Zaddy Gal."

I noticed that the marigolds and cosmos plants had tiny

buds on them. The poppies were flopping all over the place, with big fat buds in the middle of their scratchy leaves. The sunflowers were as tall as my knees. I whispered encouraging words to them all, even to the worms deep in the ground doing their slimy worm jobs.

"Maybe if we made a very loud noise, Mrs. Iptweet, we would get our neighbors' attention. Like the bullhorn. Or firecrackers. Or dynamite, if we had any."

Mrs. Iptweet moved her eyes from the sky to the garden.

She smiled and said, "That is a very creative idea, Zaady Gal. But sometimes I think there are enough loud noises in the world already, Chérie. Perhaps there is another way."

Mrs. Iptweet crouched down and ran her hand over the wispy cosmos plants. I wondered about what would be an interesting but quieter way to tell the neighborhood about our parade. I looked up at the sky. A cloud floated by way up high and an idea floated into my mind.

"What about a letter, Mrs. Iptweet?"

"A letter, Chérie?"

"Yes, Mrs. Iptweet. We could write a letter to our neighbors."

"A personal handwritten letter from you and me, Chérie, to each and every household?" Mrs. Iptweet's eyes got brighter and more twinkly. "A handwritten letter does has a lot of energy and power in it, Chérie."

"Yes, Mrs. Iptweet, and a letter is pretty quiet," I said.

"Yes, quiet and powerful and much more friendly than an explosion, Chérie."

I said, "I write interesting letters to my Aunt Belle, Mrs. Iptweet. My Aunt Belle says she loves to get my interesting letters."

"I think this is a brilliant idea, Cherie."

I said, "Thanks, Mrs. Iptweet. We could use sparkle pens to write the letters. Sparkly ink has a lot of energy and power in it, too, don't you think, Mrs. Iptweet?"

"Yes, Chérie, we will use my sparkle pens and your excellent way with words. Human beings respond well to these sorts of things, Chérie."

I said, "Yes, Mrs. Iptweet, just about everybody likes sparkle pens."

"You are right, Chérie. Personal Contact, Power and Beauty are so very important when launching a parade."

"Yes, Mrs. Iptweet. I think so."

"Let's get started, Chérie," said Mrs. Iptweet.

Mrs. Iptweet turned off the water and I put down the hose and we scooted back inside Mrs. Iptweet's studio. We each drank a gulp of coconut milk. I reached inside my pocket and pulled out my picked lettuce leaves. I put a crumpled leaf on a cracker on top of the mango jam and ate it. My concoction tasted like a lawn and a tropical garden all mixed together.

Then we got to work inspiring the neighborhood. Mrs. Iptweet and I wrote our official parade invitation letters on

Sparkly parade box

light blue paper. Light blue is the color of the sky on Midsummer's Day. It took us three days to write the thirty-one letters. We used all twenty-two of Mrs. Iptweet's sparkly glitter pens, six of my colored pencils, and four crayons. As usual, I was in charge of the words:

Dear Neighbor,

Hi, it's us, the Midsummer's Day Mythical Creature Parade Committee personally contacting you in a handwritten way. What Mythical Creature is your favorite one? Why not pick it and be it on the Longest Day of the Year, a good day to parade around. It will be an interesting day, not boring at all.

Sign up now so we know who will be in it. Leave your note in the Sign-up Box at #406. Okay?

Signed, Your Friendly Neighborly Neighbors,
The Parade Committee

Mrs. Iptweet drew dragons on her pile of letters because, in China, dragons are for good luck. I drew a mermaid on each letter in my pile because I like mermaids the best. Mermaids get to swim a lot, sit around on rocks, and eat mango jam. I like swimming, I like rocks, and I like mango jam. And I am growing my hair long, even though my mom says long hair is a bother. I bet mermaids have really interesting dreams. Plus all their friends are fish.

Mrs. Iptweet and I made the special Parade Sign-up Box out of one of Mrs. Iptweet's unpacked moving boxes. We gooped up the box with about a bucketful of glue, and poured a ton of gold glitter all over it. We also embedded the feet of seventeen tiny plastic animals into the thick sticky glue. The tiny plastic animals looked like they were parading around on the top of the glittery box. We thought for sure that this too would inspire our neighbors into a parade mood. We set the beautiful, sparkling Sign-up Box on the sidewalk in front of Mrs. Iptweet's house.

I had the idea to make a large red cardboard arrow to point exactly at the sign-up box. I taped the arrow onto Mrs. Iptweet's leafy hedge right above the box, pointing down. You couldn't miss the Sign-up Box if you tried.

We looked at our finished work and Mrs. Iptweet said, "We'll give it a week, Chérie."

On my way home from Mrs. Iptweet's that day, I walked up and down our street and put a personal parade invitation letter into every single mailbox. I had a lot of thoughts and questions swirling around in my mind. Will anybody ever want to be in this parade? Is it too weird? I wondered if my mom will be in the parade? What if my dad shows up and there is no parade? Maybe he would take me out to breakfast. I could order blueberry pancakes, three sausages, a scrambled egg, and orange soda. It has been a long time since I ate breakfast with my dad.

Usually I eat breakfast, lunch, and dinner with my mom. My mom says her only creative talent is cooking. My mom does make very interesting food. For example, for dinner my mom likes to make pancakes and tomatoes, or ravioli and peaches, or fried chicken and raisins. My mom thinks macaroni is the most perfect food of all. She can do anything with it. She makes macaroni and peanuts, macaroni and tuna fish, even macaroni and fruit salad. My personal favorite macaroni combination is macaroni and cheese.

I put the next-to-the-last letter into the mailbox at number four-twenty-four.

More thoughts swirled into my brain. What if nobody in the world cares about Midsummer's Day or Mythic Animals anymore? If nobody joins in the parade, will Mrs. Iptweet get disappointed and move away? I could not stand it if Mrs. Iptweet moved away. That would be horrible, the worst thing that could ever happen to me. But then a moment later I did think of something more horrible than that. What's going to happen when my mom finds out I am making a parade, a weird-o pretend animal parade with Mrs. Iptweet? My mom has not met Mrs. Iptweet yet. My mom might think Mrs. Iptweet is an oddball, or even worse, a crackpot. My mom does not like crackpots. And even worse than that: what about my name? My mom does not know that I told Mrs. Iptweet my name is Sheherazade. Sheherazade is not the name my mom

Food groups in a bowl

named me. These thoughts stayed in my mind and really bothered me. But my worrying got interrupted because I was home on our porch. The smells of my mom's fancy cooking floated out of our door and into my nose. I recognized the smell of my mom's famous Oatmeal Delight. She likes to make Oatmeal Delight because the ingredients – oatmeal, fruit salad, peanuts, and chocolate sprinkles – are in so many food groups. That's the Grain, Fruit, Protein, and Dessert groups all in one convenient bowl. For the Vegetable food group, my mom made Spinach Surprise – cooked spinach with butter. My health is very important to my mom.

My mom says that when I was little I was a finicky eater. Gran Modesta had a good idea to help me eat: she gave all my mom's food dishes fancy names, like Mess of Macaroni, Potatoes Mashola, Loaf of Life, Soupy Loopy, Burger of Mystery, and Bug Salad. Even when I was a small child, I liked things to have interesting names.

Mom and I sat down at the kitchen table with our steamy

bowls of Oatmeal Delight and Spinach Surprise. My mom seemed to be in a pretty good mood. Her lips were not in a straight line, and no frowny lines were on her forehead.

"How was your day, Mom?" I asked. "It smells good in here, Mom."

Then I noticed that I had the last parade invitation in my hand. Probably my mom is not interested in a stupid parade. She is too busy to come to it anyway. She will have to go grocery shopping on Midsummer's Day because Saturday is always the day for grocery shopping. I stuffed the letter into my jeans pocket fast.

"My day was fine, Darling Girl. What's that you've got there."

"What, Mom?"

"The blue paper you shoved into your pocket."

Not fast enough. Darn.

"Oh, that. Nothing important, Mom. Just some information about something you are probably not interested in, Mom."

"Really, Miss Girl?"

My mom's hands were on her hips and her face had a smile on it.

"Why not let me be the judge of what I am interested in," said my mom.

She reached over and gently slipped the crumpled blue paper out of my pocket.

I said, "Well, actually, it's a personal handwritten invitation for you, Mom, but it's not a big deal. It probably won't even happen, Mom. You have to buy groceries that day. Did you have a good day today, Mom?"

She said, "My day was fine," and read the letter. My mom scrunched up her face and looked confused. My mom does not like confusion. I could see trouble coming so I changed the subject fast.

"Hey, Mom, the Oatmeal Delight is really good tonight," I said. I stirred up the food groups in my bowl. "I like peanuts in just about anything, Mom. Thanks for making such an interesting dinner."

I smiled at her as I swallowed a spoonful.

My mom waved the letter at me and said, "What's this about, Dearie?"

"Oh, that, Mom? Um...." I scraped up a spoonful of chocolate sprinkles and ate them. My mom kept looking at me. Her eyebrows went up. There was no escape. I had to tell her.

"Mom, it's just that, um, my friend Mrs. Iptweet had a really great idea about having a parade and I'm helping her with it, Mom."

My mom's eyebrows stayed up high on her forehead.

I said, "Don't worry, Mom, I'm sure I can handle any excitement that might happen. Hey Mom, guess what? The idea for making it a Mythical Creatures theme was my very own idea. Honest, Mom."

"That's great, Kiddo," my mom said. My mom was quiet for a minute. She read the letter again. She was still frowning.

"Mom, you could be in the parade, too," I said quickly. "Everybody on the street is invited, including you. I used the tan color sparkle ink just for your letter, Mom. Tan and blue are your favorite colors, right? What Mythical Creature would you like to be, huh?"

My mom put the letter down and looked at me.

"You are spending a lot of time visiting this Mrs. Iptweet, Miss Girl. I think it's time for me to meet Mrs. Iptweet."

I choked on a glob of buttery Spinach Surprise.

"Mom," I said in a hurry after I swallowed, "Mom, don't think Mrs. Iptweet is a crackpot, Mom. She's an artist, Mom, but not a crackpot. There's a difference, Mom."

My mom rolled her eyes.

"She can't help being an artist, Mom," I said, "and her art is extremely clean and sanitary. And quiet, too. No loud noises at all, Mom."

My mom made the tsking sound with her tongue and teeth.

"That's great, but you heard me. Next Monday. I'll go with you to Mrs. Iptweet's next Monday afternoon," she said, and finished eating her bowl of Oatmeal Delight.

I wasn't hungry anymore. All my worried thoughts flooded back into my mind. About how when my mom meets Mrs. Iptweet on Monday she will see Mrs. Iptweet's flowery house and the twinkle lights on the stairway, and all Mrs. Iptweet's dolls sitting on her purple sofa. My mom will see the two hammocks hanging in the living room and the baskets of feathers. My mom will think it is too weird. And then Mrs. Iptweet will call me Sheherazade or Chérie or Zaady Gal and my mom will be all confused. And then my mom will call me by my real name, and Mrs. Iptweet will be all confused and ask my mom who she is talking about. My mom's face will scrunch up before she says, "What do you mean, Mrs. Iptweet?" It will be revealed that I am a girl who lied about her name.

I could not eat another bite of gloopy, globby Oatmeal Delight. On Monday, there was going to be trouble.

CHAPTER TEN

The Name My Mom Named Me

The next afternoon, I dragged myself to Mrs. Iptweet's garden to do my job. Probably I won't get to do it too much longer, since on Monday my world will be coming to an end. I thought this day, a Friday, might be my very last day of happiness on earth.

I got to work watering and saying encouraging words to the plants. I can adjust the spray nozzle all by myself now. The hose nozzle has a lot of choices and I have experimented with each one. JET is a hard pointy stream, too hard for delicate new plants. MIST is too soft, it only wets the leaves, not the ground where the roots are thirsty. I turn the nozzle to SHOWER a lot, because it is so much like real rain. Sometimes I use SOAK when I want to give the plants an exciting stormy hurricane experience.

Who will take care of the plants when I am fired from my

job, I thought. Does Mrs. Iptweet know all about the nozzle settings? I will have to tell Mrs. Iptweet about the best nozzle settings before she throws me off her property for lying to her about my name.

After a while Mrs. Iptweet opened her back door and came outside. She had on her red checkered shirt, her blue jeans and sequin sneakers, and her yellow apron with the ruffle on it. She was holding a long skinny paint brush in her hand.

Mrs. Iptweet said, "Oh, my. It's sunny outside, but I think I hear a real rain happening. How can that be, Sheherazade?"

Mrs. Iptweet was smiling and making a joke. I winced at the sound of my fake name.

"Hi, Mrs. Iptweet. Yep, it's the SHOWER setting," I said. I turned to her and spoke loud and clear. "This is the setting the plants like the best, Mrs. Iptweet. SHOWER. They like SHOWER much more than JET or MIST. And sometimes they appreciate the excitement of SOAK, because....." My voice trailed off.

Mrs. Iptweet stood with her hands on her hips and paint spots on her yellow apron. She looked happy. I looked down at the water showering out of the nozzle. I thought, Mrs. Iptweet has no idea I'm not who I said I am, that I am not really She-

The apron of Mrs. Iptweet

herazade, that I am a girl with a terrible name and a girl who lied. How did I get to be such a liar, I thought in my mind. I never was a liar before. What came over me on the day I met Mrs. Iptweet?

Mrs. Iptweet leaned over and peeked into my face. She smelled like paint.

"Is everything okay, Chérie?" asked Mrs. Iptweet.

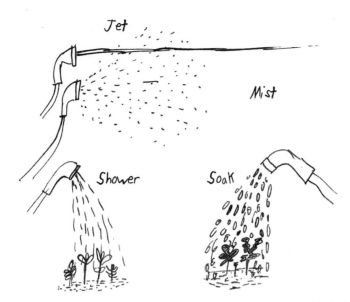

I scrunched my head down onto my chest. I couldn't look at Mrs. Iptweet.

I mumbled, "Yes, everything is okay, Mrs. Iptweet. Just great. Um, what are you painting, Mrs. Iptweet?"

Mrs. Iptweet didn't say anything for a while.

"Well, I started a canvas today. I'm not sure what it's going to be yet, but it has a lot of green and blue on it, so far."

I could see the green and blue paint specks on Mrs. Iptweet's apron. Mrs. Iptweet leaned over and pulled some weeds out of the dirt. I knew she didn't believe me that everything was okay.

"Um, Mrs. Iptweet," I said, "my mom wants to come over to meet you on Monday. But probably Monday is not a good day, right, Mrs. Iptweet?"

"Oh, that would be..."

"I know you are a very busy person, Mrs. Iptweet."

"Well, not really, Zaady..."

I interrupted Mrs. Iptweet again because a great idea popped into my mind.

I blurted it out, "I know it's too much trouble, Mrs. Iptweet! I can tell my mom you won't be here, Mrs. Iptweet. Yeah, that's it. I'll tell my mom that you had to leave the country for an unexpected emergency, Mrs. Iptweet. My mom won't mind at all. My mom understands about emergencies, Mrs. Iptweet. She has math emergencies at work a lot. Math emergencies happen to bookkeepers all the time. And once, when I was five, I unexpectedly stepped on a rusty nail. The sharp nail went right through my shoe into the bottom of my foot, Mrs. Iptweet. My mom had to rush me to the hospital emergency room, unexpectedly. I had to get a lot of shots. I cried and everything. It was terrible. So my mom will understand about Monday, Mrs. Iptweet."

Mrs. Iptweet looked at my face for a minute.

"Chérie, I'd like very much to meet your mother. I'm not too busy on Monday. Monday will be fine."

Mrs. Iptweet pulled another weed out of the ground.

"That rusty nail must have hurt like the dickens, Zaady Gal."

Did Mrs. Iptweet have to keep saying my fake-o name? Why is Mrs. Iptweet tormenting me? I couldn't stand it. My knees felt all wobbly because my interesting life was crumbling apart. When Mrs. Iptweet finds out the truth about my name she will probably call me a big fat liar and tell me to get off her land. What will my mom say when she finds out I named myself a new name? Probably she will kick me out of our family and call the police. After I get out of the slammer, I will need a plane ticket to go to Aunt Belle's house, except I don't know the way to the airport.

These thoughts were heavy inside my head. My thoughts were so heavy my neck couldn't hold up my head anymore. My head flopped down in front of me; my chin smacked onto my chest.

But Aunt Belle understands about names. I know my Aunt Belle will take me in. Maybe my dad could ride me on his motorcycle to Aunt Belle's house. We will have to pack a lot of lunches for when we ride through areas where there are no restaurants. Except there's no room on the motorcycle for a hundred sandwiches in a cooler. I'll have to hold the cooler on my lap. But my lap is too small, and how will I hold onto my dad's belt loops and the cooler at the same time? Oh no, my dad and I will starve. We'll die in the desert. I'll die missing my mom and calling out for root beer and my mom's amazing yummy Macaroni and Cheese.

But maybe there will be restaurants in the desert, I thought. Maybe I will live, and maybe it will be fun at Aunt Belle's. I could dig a garden in back of Aunt Belle's house and plant stuff. I wonder if Aunt Belle has any worms in her dirt. Aunt Belle has a lot of rusty trash, but no sparkle pens. And even if she did have sparkle pens, it still will never be the same without Mrs. Iptweet. I will really miss Mrs. Iptweet.

Mrs. Iptweet's voice startled me.

She said, "Sheherazade, is anything wrong? Are you worried about something?"

I was looking down at the ground. I knew I had to tell Mrs. Iptweet the truth.

"Mrs. Iptweet, Sheherazade is not my real name," I mumbled.

"Excuse me, Chérie, I didn't hear you."

I took a big deep breath.

"Sheherazade is not my real name, Mrs. Iptweet. I have a different name."

"Really?" Mrs. Iptweet said. "A different name, Chérie?"

"Yes, Mrs. Iptweet."

"Oh," said Mrs. Iptweet.

"Um, my mom didn't name me Sheherazade. My mom gave me a different name at birth. It's a really boring name."

Mrs. Iptweet put her chin in her hands.

I said, "My mom was really tired out after having me and she wasn't thinking straight at the time."

"Yes, giving birth can tire a person out. I remember."

"Also, my mom had no experience with naming anyone before me."

"It is a challenge to name someone you just met."

We were quiet for a minute. So far, Mrs. Iptweet had not yelled at me. She didn't seem angry.

"And what name did your mother give you, Chérie?" asked Mrs. Iptweet.

I closed my eyes and breathed in a big breath.

"Prudence," I said.

I opened my eyes. Then I saw Mrs. Iptweet open her eyes wide.

"When I was five minutes old my mom named me Prudence. Pretty bad, huh?" I asked.

"Well, Prudence is a big name. A big name is a challenge for a child. A big name is grown into," said Mrs. Iptweet.

"My last name is boring, too, Mrs. Iptweet. Hornby. My last name is Hornby."

Mrs. Iptweet scratched her nose, and scrunched up her eyes.

"Prudence Hornby. Well, it has a ring to it, Chérie."

"I don't think so, Mrs. Iptweet."

"Well,…" said Mrs. Iptweet, but I interrupted her.

"Mrs. Iptweet, there's more."

"Oh?"

"My middle name, Mrs. Iptweet. You better brace yourself, Mrs. Iptweet."

Mrs. Iptweet braced herself.

"Okay. I'm ready," she said.

"Fish, Mrs. Iptweet. My middle name is Fish."

Mrs. Iptweet blinked.

"Fish? F, I, S, H? Fish?" she asked.

"Yes, F, I, S, H," I said.

"That is a very unique middle name."

"It's because my mom likes dolphins a lot. My mom says dolphins are intelligent and happy fish."

Mrs. Iptweet said, "Oh, I see."

"But then, in second grade, I found out that a dolphin is not a fish; a dolphin is a mammal. I can't tell my mom because she might decide to be exact and I could not stand to have my middle name be Mammal."

"I agree," said Mrs. Iptweet. "Fish is better."

"So, Mrs. Iptweet, Prudence Fish Hornby is my real name."

We sat there quietly for a moment. Mrs. Iptweet put her chin in her hand.

"Well, Chérie…"

I interrupted Mrs. Iptweet. "Do you want to me get off your land now, Mrs. Iptweet? I'll understand completely. I lied to you about my true identity. I'm really sorry, Mrs. Iptweet."

"Chérie,…" said Mrs. Iptweet.

Tears slipped out of my eyes before I could stop them. Big wet drips slid down my cheeks. I sort of choked and sobbed out the words, "But I don't feel like a Prudence Fish Hornby, Mrs. Iptweet. I feel like a Sheherazade."

Mrs. Iptweet pulled a red flowery hankie out of her apron pocket. She reached over and wiped my face. I blew my nose into the red hankie. This was the second time I had filled a fancy hankie of Mrs. Iptweet's with my nose goop.

Mrs. Iptweet was quiet for a minute.

"Thank you for telling me, Chérie," said Mrs. Iptweet. "That took a lot of courage."

"Should I leave now, Mrs. Iptweet?" I asked.

Mrs. Iptweet put the wet hankie back into her pocket.

"Zaady Gal, I have a better idea. I think now is a good time to talk about the about the Magic and Power of Names. Shall we?"

She pulled me up by both hands and led the way into her studio.

CHAPTER ELEVEN

The Magic and Power of Names

Inside the studio was cool and dark. I smelled the smell of paint and turpentine. Mrs. Iptweet's newest painting sat on a bench, leaning against the wall. Her rocking chair with the swirls, hearts and dots painted on it was sitting in front of the painting. Mrs. Iptweet likes to rock and paint at the same time.

Mrs. Iptweet motioned to me to sit on the blue and white stripey cushiony chair.

"Be careful, Chérie, there are some paint drips on that chair," said Mrs. Iptweet. "I don't know how those drips landed there. It seems paint has a mind of its own."

I climbed into the comfy chair and sat in between the paint blobs. Mrs. Iptweet pulled out a big fat book from her bookcase. She turned her rocking chair to face me and sat down.

"So, the Magic and Power of Names. Ready?" asked Mrs. Iptweet.

"Yes, I'm ready, Mrs. Iptweet," I said. "Thanks for not kicking me off your land, Mrs. Iptweet."

Mrs. Iptweet shook her head.

"You have a wild mind, Chérie."

"Do you really think so, Mrs. Iptweet?" I asked.

Mrs. Iptweet nodded her head and fluffed her hair.

"Names," said Mrs. Iptweet. "For some people, Chérie, their Birth name and their Real name are the same."

Mrs. Iptweet looked at my eyes to make sure I heard her.

"But for other people, Chérie, their Real name is different from their Birth name."

"Oh," I said.

Mrs. Iptweet opened up the big fat book and paged through it.

"Let's take a close look at your birth name, Chérie. You are one of the few people whose name can be found in a dictionary, so we can easily find out its meaning and root."

"Mrs. Iptweet, my Gran Modesta and I read through the dictionary a lot of times. Prudence means cautious behavior, Mrs. Iptweet." I said. I shrugged my shoulders. "Pretty boring."

Mrs. Iptweet said, "Yes, cautious behavior is one interpretation of the word prudence, Prudence."

Mrs. Iptweet smiled at me.

"I have to practice saying your birth name, Chérie."

I watched Mrs. Iptweet's finger move down the page of the dictionary, then stop.

"Here it is," she said.

I got up off the comfy chair and stood next to Mrs. Iptweet and the dictionary. Mrs. Iptweet's sparkly red fingernail pointed exactly to the word prudence.

"Prudence," said Mrs. Iptweet. "From the medieval French language."

Mrs. Iptweet closed her eyes. "Oh, Chérie. France. La belle France," she said. "France is a beautiful country, Chérie, full of interesting people. And French is a language full of beautiful words."

Oh wow, my name comes from France, I thought.

Mrs. Iptweet kept reading.

"Prudence. Derived from the word Providence. The power that sustains and guides humans on earth."

"I don't know what that means, Mrs. Iptweet," I said.

Mrs. Iptweet looked up at me.

"It means you are a born leader, Zaady Gal." Mrs. Iptweet patted my shoulder. "It says right here, Chérie, prudence is also the word for good judgment. Prudence is an aspect of wisdom."

Mrs. Iptweet closed the dictionary.

"There is much more to the word and name Prudence, Chérie, than cautious behavior. It is a big name, Chérie, with a lot of power to it."

"But, Mrs. Iptweet, it didn't say anything about adventure or excitement."

Mrs. Iptweet shook her head.

"No. But I think a name that means 'guiding human destiny' and has its root in France could open the way for many adventures, Chérie."

Mrs. Iptweet put the dictionary back on the shelf.

She said, "And you've got your last name, too, Chérie. Hornby. Horns are important instruments for the heralding of good news and for announcing important information, Chérie."

Hmmm, I thought. "Like maybe announcing a warning about a dangerous situation? Like maybe that an earthquake is happening?"

Mrs. Iptweet smiled. "Yes, exactly, Chérie."

I sat back down on the paint-spattered chair. I said, "What about my middle name, Mrs. Iptweet? Fish. Fish are slimy, wet and smelly."

Mrs. Iptweet laughed out loud.

"Wet and slimy is one way to think about fish, Chérie," said Mrs. Iptweet. "But fish can be exquistely beautiful."

"That's true, Mrs. Iptweet. I did have a very beautiful goldfish when I was five."

"And, Chérie, Fish, like every creature on earth, is a Sacred Being with its own special gifts to give."

"Oh. Right, Mrs. Iptweet."

"Fish is nourishment for all parts of the body, including the brain."

I said, "I like my mom's macaroni and tuna fish, Mrs. Iptweet."

"And throughout the ages, Fish has been a symbol for Dreaming and telling Deep Truths, Chérie."

"I had the dream about the cloud-patting girl, Mrs. Iptweet, and the talking stones, remember?"

"Yes, I do, Chérie. A truly magnificent and epic dream,"

Mrs. Iptweet said. "I think that your birth name, Prudence Fish Hornby, is a perfectly fine name for a lovely, word-loving, adventurous, dreaming girl like you, Sheherazade."

I wondered why Mrs. Iptweet was still calling me Sheherazade, my fake-o name.

Mrs. Iptweet walked around her studio and sat on the stool near the big art table. She looked me straight in the eye.

"Chérie, I think Sheherazade is your Secret Power Name."

I blinked.

"Do you think so, Mrs. Iptweet?" I asked. "What is a Secret Power Name, exactly?"

"It's the name that tells about a person's special talents, Chérie, a person's special powers."

"Oh," I said.

"Chérie, in a few parts of the world a baby is given a secret power name, as well as the family name, when it is born."

I said, "That's pretty interesting, Mrs. Iptweet."

"The mother deeply senses who her baby is and whispers its power name into her newborn baby's ear."

My eyes got very wide and big because I was surprised and shocked to hear this.

"Really, Mrs. Iptweet?"

"Then all through the child's life, the child can call on the power of its secret name whenever strength or inspiration or courage is needed."

I didn't say anything. I was quiet.

Mrs. Iptweet said, "And it's also true that a person can choose her own secret power name."

A swirly feeling started swirling around inside me.

I asked Mrs. Iptweet, "What do I do now, Mrs. Iptweet?"

"I think we get the teacups and some tea and we have a toast to welcome your name in an official way."

Mrs. Iptweet and I ran upstairs to her pink kitchen. We made a pot of cinnamon orange tea, a flavor that Sheherazade of Arabia would have tasted and enjoyed long ago.

Bluebird teacups

Mrs. Iptweet lifted up her bluebird teacup and said, "To the brave and creative Sheherazade, who told stories which are not forgotten."

I clinked my teacup onto Mrs. Iptweet's and said, "Yaaay."

"And to Prudence Fish Hornby, secretly and powerfully known as Sheherazade."

We clinked teacups again.

"How do you feel, Prudence?"

I said, "Pretty swirly, Mrs. Iptweet."

Mrs. Iptweet put her hand on my shoulder.

"The Magic and Power of Names can do that, Chérie."

After a few sips of the spicy tea, the other problem about my Secret Power Name came into my mind. I put down my teacup.

"Mrs. Iptweet, my mom does not know about my Sheherazade name yet."

Mrs. Iptweet said, "Hmmm."

"Mrs. Iptweet, when my mom comes to meet you on Monday, she will hear you call me Sheherazade. My mom will not know who you are talking to, Mrs. Iptweet, and maybe she will think you have an imaginary friend that we don't see."

Mrs. Iptweet nodded her head.

"My mom doesn't believe in imaginary friends for grownups, Mrs. Iptweet," I said. "It could be a real problem, Mrs. Iptweet."

"I see what you mean, Prudence," said Mrs. Iptweet. "On Monday, when your mom comes to visit, Prudence, there will be no confusion. I will call you Prudence, Prudence."

Mrs. Iptweet was practicing remembering my name to get ready for the visit of my mom.

"It will be a pleasure to honor the name your mom named you, Prudence." Mrs. Iptweet smiled. "And, Prudence, I am sure the right moment will arrive when you can share with your mom about your Secret Power Name."

"Thanks, Mrs. Iptweet," I said. "Yeah, I'll tell her someday, at exactly the right moment."

Mrs. Iptweet stood up.

"How about papaya juice and a coconut cake for our visit on Monday, Chérie? Do you think your mom would enjoy that?"

"Yes, Mrs. Iptweet," I said. "My mom likes fancy food. She makes fancy food all the time."

"We will have a tasty time on Monday."

Mrs. Iptweet pointed to her painting on the bench.

"What do you think about this painting so far, Chérie? What do you see?"

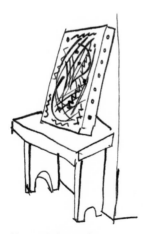

Mrs. Iptweet's new painting

I looked at the wavy blue lines, the green dots and swooshes, and the dark purple swirls.

I said, "It looks like the bottom of a deep blue sea to me, Mrs. Iptweet. And there is a mermaid with long blue hair."

I pointed to a bunch of blue lines in the middle.

Mrs. Iptweet leaned her head sideways.

"Yes," she said. "I can see her, Chérie."

Mrs. Iptweet looked at me.

"I think all our talk about mermaids lately is showing up in this painting."

Mrs. Iptweet leaned her head the other way.

"When I lean my head this way, Chérie, it looks to me like a fierce rainstorm in a forest." Mrs. Iptweet likes to paint first and decide what it is later.

"It could be a forest, Mrs. Iptweet," I said. "But...." I pointed to a big green wavy shape. "This looks like a whale's tail to me, Mrs. Iptweet."

"Oh, yes," said Mrs. Iptweet. "You have a good eye for form, Chérie."

She picked up a long skinny paintbrush and swirled it around in a glob of red paint.

"I think this painting needs some red, Chérie," said Mrs. Iptweet. "What do you think?"

"Yes. Red is a great color, Mrs. Iptweet. Probably mermaids like red."

Mrs. Iptweet smiled and said, "Have you been thinking of what Mythic Creature you want to be in the parade?"

"I really like Mythic Mermaids, Mrs. Iptweet. They have long hair and my hair is growing pretty fast."

"Mythic Mermaid is a great idea, Chérie. You would be an enchanting Mermaid."

"Thanks, Mrs. Iptweet."

"There is another very important part to be played on Parade Day, Chérie. A crucial part."

I said, "Oh?"

"The Mythical Creatures Parade must have someone to be the symbol of where Mythical Creatures come from, Chérie."

I looked up.

"You mean a book, Mrs. Iptweet? You want someone to dress up like a book?"

"Not exactly, Chérie. Do you remember where the stories first came from before they were written into books, or onto papyrus or onto rocks, Chérie?"

I remembered where the stories came from.

"From inspirations in the olden people's Artist Minds, Mrs. Iptweet. The olden people told the stories out loud to their friends. Right, Mrs. Iptweet?"

Mrs. Iptweet nodded her head.

"I think it is quite a coincidence that you and the brave story-teller, Sheherazade of Arabia, share a name together," said Mrs. Iptweet. "Would you consider portraying the Mythic Story-teller, Chérie, in the parade?"

I thought about that for a moment.

I said, "Well, I'll consider it, Mrs. Iptweet."

Mrs. Iptweet smiled and turned to her painting.

"See you on Monday, Miss Prudence. No worries," said Mrs. Iptweet.

CHAPTER TWELVE

I Cheer up My Mom, Sort Of

At home that afternoon, I smelled the smell of macaroni and cheese, my all-time favorite macaroni food. I set the table with our blue plates. They are plain pale blue and they break easily. We have four plates left, but this is not a problem because we only need two plates each night. I set out the forks, the knives, and the spoons. My mom likes me to set out all three types of eating tools, whether we need them all or not. Sometimes the spoons just lay there doing nothing, but my mom says we have standards.

While I set the table, I kept having thoughts. What about my being the Mythic Storyteller in our parade? I was really counting on being a Mythic Mermaid. A mermaid costume is very interesting and my hair is getting longer each day.

Being the Mythic Storyteller sounds like a big job. Will I have to tell a mythic story? I am not very experienced at telling mythic stories. But if I did portray the Mythic Storyteller, I could wear a Sheherazade costume. Gran told me Sheherazade of Arabia wore very fancy and sparkly clothes almost all the time. Probably Sherazade had long hair, too, and used many different kinds of exotic barrettes in her fancy hairdos.

If Mrs. Iptweet and I are the only ones in our parade, it will be very important for our costumes to be extremely interesting-looking. I did tell stories with Gran Modesta. And Gran liked my stories. And my Secret Power Name is Sheherazade.

I set out our blue paper napkins, and a couple of glasses. I like to drink root beer when I eat macaroni and cheese. My mom likes plain water.

My mom and I sat down at the table. My mom scooped out a big pile of macaroni and cheese onto my plate. For a moment, the steamy cheesy smell took away all my thoughts and questions.

I said, "Oh wow, Mom, this is so great. Macaroni and cheese is my favorite macaroni food. Yum, Mom."

My mom was pretty quiet and her eyes were all puffy and red again. But she smiled at me and put some food on her own plate and sat down.

"I'm glad you like it, Darling Girl," said my mom.

She passed me the Spinach Surprise which tastes good with everything and is two food groups in one: Vegetable and Dairy.

Sometimes Friday nights are still sad for my mom because Friday was the night Gran Modesta came over for dinner each week. I wished I could cheer up my mom.

Probably hearing about my Secret Power Name would not do that.

After another bite of macaroni and cheese, I said, "Hey Mom, Mrs. Iptweet is making some fancy food for you on Monday. I think you will like it."

My mom looked up from her plate.

"My goodness, I hope she's not going to a lot of trouble. It's going to be a short visit. I just want to meet her, and make sure she's not a nut or something."

Oh well. That didn't work.

"You will see that she is not a nut, Mom. Mrs. Iptweet is really a nice person, Mom."

My mom said. "I'm sure she is."

My mom and I kept eating our yummy food. My mom took a deep breath and sighed. "I'm sorry to be a little low tonight, Prudy. And I'm sorry not to have Bug Salad for you."

Gran Modesta always brought Bug Salad on Friday nights. My mom invented Bug Salad, and Gran Modesta named it. Bug Salad is made out of tomatoes, cucumbers, and raisins. Gran always said someday our Bug Salad would become world famous. So far, that has not happened because Bug Salad does not have a great taste.

"Oh, that's okay, Mom," I said. "I love macaroni and cheese, Mom. Don't worry about it at all, Mom. Really."

"That's nice of you to say, Prudy, but I'll make it again next Friday. I just couldn't face Bug Salad tonight without Gran." My mom got quiet again.

I ate more macaroni and cheese. It tasted good in my mouth, warm, gooey and salty. A lot of thoughts came into my mind. I wondered who made this good food for the very first time. How did macaroni and cheese get invented anyhow? I ate another spoonful. I remembered how much fun it was when Gran came to dinner on Fridays. Gran liked macaroni and cheese, too. After dinner, Gran and I would go upstairs and read or tell stories.

Just then an idea came into my mind about how I might be able to cheer up my mom.

I swallowed. I said, "Hey, Mom, do you want to hear a story?" She sighed and said, "Sure, Prudy."

I put my spoon down and wiped the cheese off my mouth.

"This is a story about the very first macaroni and cheese dinner."

"Okay. Tell me," said my mom.

"A long time ago, Mom, high up on a hill, there was a girl, Mom. Um, she was patting a small cloud that was made of cheese. And at the bottom of the hill, lots of goats were running through a field of wheat plants."

"Is this something you read about in school today?" my mom asked.

"Um, no, Mom," I said. "I'm making it up. Okay, Mom?"

My mom said, "Okay. Go on."

"Well, a whole big bunch of chickens were lounging around the hill, too, pecking at seeds and grit. Chickens love grit, Mom. Everything was great, no problems were happening at all. Everybody was relaxed. But then, it was shocking, Mom, a giant huge hurricane stormed into the hill and valley place. It was so windy and loud! The chickens got so scared they laid eggs all over everywhere. The goats were running around in terror and broke up all the eggs."

I was really liking the story, so I kept going. My mom did not interrupt me.

"Mom, the heavy rain pushed down the wheat plants, and the goats stepped on the wheat plants and crushed them real bad. The big fat drops of rain soaked everything into a big messy mess. And the cloud-patting girl was yelling because the cheese blew out of her hands and was whipping all around the sky in the clutches of the Stupendous Hurricane of Windiness!"

"It seemed like all was lost, and life on the hill was com-

pletely over. But no! Life was definitely not over on that hill, Mom. The girl shouted, 'Cut it out Wind, stop trying to scare me! It won't work! I have better things to do than be afraid of you!'"

Then a really good idea popped into my mind.

I said, "Mom, the cloud-patting girl put her hands over her head and pointed right at the storm, Mom. She yelled, 'I am Sheherazade. Yes, that is me. I now use my Secret Power Name to tame you, Stupendous Hurricane. I command you to stop making this mess right now, says I, the mighty Sheherazade.'"

"This girl had a special secret power name, Mom, that she used whenever she got into a tough situation, Mom."

My mom's eyes were wide open. She was chewing her Spinach Surprise and could not say anything with her mouth all full. I kept going, because the story was so exciting now.

"In a minute the Stormy Storm stopped, Mom, and quietly went on its way. The hurricane felt bad about messing everything up, so in order to apologize to the cloud-patting girl and the animals, the Stormy Hurricane left them a present. Guess what it was, Mom."

My mom shrugged her shoulders and shook her head. My mom did not know what the present could be.

"Mom," I said. "The mess of rain and broken eggs and crushed wheat plants were magically transformed into macaroni! And the big cloud of cheese fell to earth exactly at the right place in order to blend in perfectly. All around on the ground was macaroni and cheese, Mom! Everybody had a feast of the amazing combination of tastes, for the very first time."

I stopped for a minute. I decided that was the end of the story.

I said, "The end, Mom."

My mom put down her fork. She gave a short laugh and looked at me funny. I hoped I didn't scare her too much with the storm part.

She asked, "You made that up, Prudy?"

I said, "Yes, Mom. Was the storm part too scary for you?"

"Is it a myth or something?"

I said, "No, Mom. It's not a myth, Mom. I did dream about the cloud-patting girl once. And I really like the taste of macaroni and cheese, Mom."

My mom's eyes got all full of tears and she started to cry. I thought maybe my mom was sad that the eggs got broken at the end. She said no, it was not the eggs. It was that Gran Modesta had an imaginative mind, too, and could make up a story in a minute.

"Prudy, you remind me so much of your Gran," my mom said.

My mom came over to my chair and gave me a big squeezy wet hug. She said what a great story that was, and she can hardly believe I made it up right there, and I am so creative and so good with words and stories, just like my Gran.

"Do you think so, Mom? Really?" I asked. My face was wet with my mom's tears.

"Without a doubt, Prudence. Since you were very small I noticed it."

"Gran and I did a lot of reading together, Mom."

"Gran read to me a lot, too, Prudence, when I was a little girl. In those days my mother worked so hard. We read only at night, at bedtime, and we'd fall asleep together. But I never could make up a story all by myself."

I tried to picture my mom when she was a girl like me, sleeping in a bed with her mom.

My mom gave me another hug. Then she picked up our two blue plates and carried them over to the sink. When my mom carries the plates to the sink, I know it is time for me to wash the dishes. I pulled a chair over to the sink and put two pink rubber gloves onto my hands.

My mom said, "Yes. No doubt about it. Prudence, you have a gift."

I stood on the chair and turned on the hot water. I let a lot of hot water run into the washbasin and squeezed a gigantic green blob of dishwash soap under the stream of water. When I wash dishes I like there to be about a million bubbles. My mom brought the glasses and utensils and dumped them into the sudsy washbasin. My mom picked up her broom and started to sweep the floor. My mom sweeps the floor every night whether it needs it or not.

"Let's have some dessert tonight, Prudence. I think your story calls for some dessert."

The plate I was washing dropped out of my hand into the dishpan, but did not break.

I said, "That's a great idea, Mom."

"Let's go get ice cream at the Hullaballoo. Cones with sprinkles, okay?" asked my mom.

After the dishes were washed and the floor swept, my mom and I drove a short way in our blue car to the Hullaballoo Ice Cream Emporium. There are about two hundred and seven

different flavors of ice cream at the Hullaballoo. I ordered my favorite kind. My mom ordered vanilla with chocolate sprinkles.

"Let's find a table, Prudence. You choose."

I picked the small round table near the window. This table has a surfer dude painted on it and it is right next to the pretend palm tree. I like the strings of flamingo lights that hang on the plastic tree. I sat on the hot pink chair. My mom sat on the orange chair with black tiger stripes. My mom says she is willing to overlook Mr. Hullaballoo's terrible taste in decorating, because he makes great vanilla ice cream.

It was pretty crowded in the Hullaballoo. My mom and I sat and licked our cones.

My mom smiled and said, "I liked your story, Prudence."

"Thanks, Mom," I said. "What part of the story did you like the best, Mom?"

"I think I liked all of it, Prudy." Mom licked the chocolate sprinkles off one side of her cone.

"Wow. Thanks, Mom," I said. Maybe now is the exact right moment, I thought.

"Hey Mom, did you notice how the girl in my story had a Secret Power Name, Mom?"

"Yes, I did, Prudence. That was an interesting twist, I thought."

"Secret Power Names can come in really handy during life, Mom. I really like the Sheherazade name, Mom. Don't you?"

My Mom shot me a look over her ice cream.

"It's okay, I guess," she said.

"I think it is a beautiful name, Mom. You know, Mom, I wouldn't mind having the name Sheherazade for my very own name, Mom. That's how much I like it."

"That's very interesting, Prudence," my mom said.

"You could call me Chérie for short, Mom. Wouldn't that be convenient?"

My mom took a bite of her vanilla ice cream and let it melt in her mouth.

"Yes, I guess I could call you Chérie. I don't know how convenient it would be. But I probably won't be calling you Chérie because your name is definitely not Sheherazade. Is it?"

I looked at my mom and took another lick of my blueberry chocolate fudge supreme with red cinnamon sprinkles ice cream cone. I bet the real Sheherazade would have ordered this exact flavor for herself.

"No, not exactly, Mom."

My mom wiped her mouth with her paper napkin.

"What are you getting at, Prudy? You're not wanting to change your name to Sheherazade, are you?"

She put her cone down onto the tiny white plate Mr. Hullaballoo gave us to use in case we had an ice cream emergency.

My mom made the tsking sound and said, "It's your Aunt Belle putting ideas into your head, I just know it."

"No, Mom, Aunt Belle..."

My mom kept talking. "I know you've never liked the name I gave you, Prudence. But I'm sorry, you are much too young to change your name. I won't hear of it, Prudence, do you understand?"

"Mom," I said. "It's really..."

My mom interrupted me again. She was getting pretty worked up.

"Prudence is a perfectly lovely name. Someday you will come to appreciate it and then you will thank me for giving you a name with integrity and strength. Prudence is not just any old name, you know."

"No, Mom, it's not just any old name. It's French, Mom, it means..."

"And anyway, I was trying to honor my mother when I chose it. Prudence is a virtue, too, like Modesty."

"Mom..." I said.

"It's really rather reckless, Prudence, everybody changing their name at the drop of a hat. It took me forever to call Belle, Belle and not Edith, and Edith is a perfectly fine name. I don't know why she did that. Just to annoy her family..."

I have a really loud voice when I need it, just like my mom does.

I yelled, "MOM, I HAVE A SECRET POWER NAME AND IT'S SHEHERAZADE, MOM."

My mom heard me that time, but so did everybody else at the Hullaballoo Ice Cream Emporium. It got really quiet and everybody looked at us. My mom stopped talking for a minute. Then she said, "Excuse me?"

"Mom, I discovered all about Secret Power Names and, guess what, I have one."

My mom looked at me.

"You could have a Secret Power Name, too, Mom, if you want one. I could help you think it up, Mom."

I explained to my mom everything I learned about names, except the part about dolphins being mammals, not fish.

"So, Mom, I don't want to change my name completely, I just want to add to my name, secretly."

"Oh. I see. Thank you, Prudence, for explaining," my mom said. "I think I understand."

My mom wiped her hands on the napkin.

"I guess there is no harm in your having an imaginary name. You are still a young girl."

My mom's face got softer looking. She used her plastic spoon to scoop up a taste of her melty ice cream. "You can have your secret name but I will continue to call you Prudence. You have an imaginative mind, and I guess I have to expect this kind of thing."

I said, "Thanks for understanding, Mom."

My mom rolled her eyes, shook her head, patted my arm, then leaned over and kissed my forehead.

That night I got all comfy and settled in my Dream-o-rama and I wrote a letter to my Aunt Belle.

Dear Aunt Belle,
   I am going to be the Mythic Storyteller in the parade. I have a Secret Power Name. I am not lying. What Mythical Creature is your favorite one?
                  Love from your niece, Prudy
                  (Sheherazade)

CHAPTER THIRTEEN

My Mom Meets Mrs. Iptweet

On Monday afternoon, my mom was waiting for me at home. I dumped my book bag on the living room floor and we set out for Mrs. Iptweet's house right away.

"I haven't taken a walk in so long," my mom said.

We walked down the street and my mom noticed our parade handiwork.

"What are all these flapping papers on the trees, Prudence?" she asked me.

"Tsk, tsk," she said.

"Oh, Mom. These are the signs Mrs. Iptweet and I made, Mom."

I ran up to one tree and pointed out the words on the flapping signs so my mom could see what a good job I did.

"I wrote the words by myself, Mom, but so far no one has signed up to be in the parade."

My mom read the sign.

"Very interesting, Prudy," she said.

I could see my mom wanted to roll her eyes, but she pursed her lips instead.

We walked the rest of the way down our street without saying anything. I had nervous feelings in my stomach, so I skipped ahead of my mom. The air was full of June smells, and the trees were leafy. Sometimes skipping helps to calm my stomach, but not today. Today my stomach was full of flapping butterflies. I kept wondering what will happen when my mom and Mrs. Iptweet meet. What will happen when my mom sees Mrs. Iptweet's oddball house?

"You will see a lot of unusual things in Mrs. Iptweet's house, Mom," I said. "I think it's part of her being an artist and all, Mom. Like Aunt Belle, only more clean and tidy. Mrs. Iptweet is clean and tidy like you are, Mom."

"Yes, I am sure she is, Prudence," my mom said. She kept walking.

Maybe my mom will disagree with Mrs. Iptweet about something and they will have an argument, I thought. My mom can yell very loud when she gets upset.

"You know, Mom, sometimes I like to learn new ideas from people I don't know. Don't you? Sometimes it is really interesting. Like when that computer man came to my school, Mom. His brand of computer is not the same as ours, and ours is better, but I didn't mind hearing him. I didn't need to yell at him or anything just for thinking his computer brand was better."

"You are very broad-minded, Prudence," said my mom. She was walking ahead of me now. My legs were not working that great.

Maybe my mom will not like Mrs. Iptweet's papaya juice or coconut cake. We never have papaya juice at home, and my mom only makes vanilla cakes with chocolate icing. I hope Mrs. Iptweet has cheese and crackers in the kitchen, just in case. My mom always likes cheese and crackers.

At Mrs. Iptweet's house, number four-o-six, I stopped.

"Here we are, Mom. This house is Mrs. Iptweet's house, right here. Number four-o-six. Yep, here we are, Mom."

My mom walked up and I stumbled up the front walkway, past Mrs. Iptweet's peachy-pink azalea bushes, and up Mrs. Iptweet's two steps onto her porch. My mom and I stood there on the porch. I couldn't seem to move my legs anymore. My legs were frozen still, but my mouth worked okay.

I said, "See Mrs. Iptweet's doorbell, Mom? See how she painted it all polka dots? Isn't that interesting and unusual, Mom?"

I pointed to the doorbell.

What if my mom says I cannot work or play at Mrs. Iptweet's garden anymore? How will I be able to go on? I won't be able to go on, that's what. I will have to sneak out of our house every afternoon and quietly tiptoe, or crawl, along the sidewalk and across the street. There are several bushy bushes I could run between and use as camouflage until I am safely across the street and in the back alleyway. I will have to be careful about not scratching my knees or tearing my jeans while I am scrambling through the underbrush on our street. I hope I do not come across any prickly thorny plants on my way. Prickles and thorns could be big problems. My mom would notice if any part of me was bleeding. Then my mom would definitely know something was going on. Probably she'd lock our front door and put the key in her pocket or maybe under the sofa cushion where she takes her nap every afternoon. I would have to think up another daring escape plan.

"Ring the bell, Prudy, please," said my mom.

My mom was looking around at Mrs. Iptweet's porch. I watched my mom's eyes see Mrs. Iptweet's red, blue, green, purple, and white hammock swinging between the porch posts. My mom saw Mrs. Iptweet's baskets of interesting leaves and grasses and the seashells in a row along the front edge of the porch. Then my mom looked up and saw the birdcages hanging from the porch ceiling. Mrs. Iptweet leaves the tiny birdcage doors wide open all the time so that visiting birds can come and go as they please.

I said, "Mom, this is a fun-looking porch, don't you think? And it's pretty neat and clean, too, Mom, even though it is full of stuff, huh, Mom?"

My mom leaned over and whispered in my ear, "You can relax, Prudence. I've been around artists before."

I whispered back, "Oh, right, Mom."

I tried to make a smile on my face, but my nervous feelings got in the way.

I pushed the doorbell button. We heard the ding-dong sound happening inside Mrs. Iptweet's house. We heard Mrs. Iptweet's footsteps coming towards the door. Then it was Mrs. Iptweet opening the door wide and pushing open the screen door for us.

"Good afternoon, Ladies," Mrs. Iptweet said. "Please come in."

My mouth fell open. I stood there and stared at Mrs. Iptweet. Her long, curly red hair was floating all around her face. I could see her long earrings through her hair: lavender, pink and red beads dangling all the way to her shoulders. She was wearing a long white lacy dress, with a purple sequined belt around her waist. On her feet were red shoes. And on Mrs. Iptweet's smiling lips was red red lipstick.

My mom gave me a little push. I closed my mouth and

stepped inside into Mrs. Iptweet's yellow living room. Mrs. Iptweet took my mom's hand in her own hands.

"Such a pleasure to meet you, Mrs. Hornby."

My mom said, "Thank you, Mrs. Iptweet. It's nice to meet you, too."

"Hi, there, *Prudence*," said Mrs. Iptweet, and she winked at me.

I smiled back at Mrs. Iptweet because I can't make a wink happen yet in either one of my eyes, especially when I am extremely nervous.

"Please have a seat, you two," said Mrs. Iptweet.

My mom and I sat down on Mrs. Iptweet's fuzzy purple sofa. I sat next to the heart and stars pillow, near the dolls. My mom sat next to the bird and flowers pillow. Mrs. Iptweet sat on her velvety dark blue chair. In between the chair and sofa was Mrs. Iptweet's coffee table. Her coffee table is made out of two large square rocks holding up a slab of flat pink stone. On the stony table was sitting Mrs. Iptweet's big blue glass pitcher and a tray with three blue glasses, three small bluebird plates, and three forks. Beside the tray was a gigantic white cake. It looked like a fluffy white cloud resting on the flat stone tabletop in Mrs. Iptweet's living room.

"Mrs. Hornby, would you like some papaya juice? A piece of coconut cake?" asked Mrs. Iptweet.

My mom said, "Thank you, Mrs. Iptweet. This is very nice of you. I just wanted to stop by and introduce myself. You've gone to a lot of trouble, I see."

Mrs. Iptweet cut the cake and poured orange-colored juice into all the glasses.

"Oh no, it is no trouble at all, Mrs. Hornby. I am so glad you are here. It is such a pleasure to meet the mother of Prudence."

Mrs. Iptweet smiled at me. Mrs. Iptweet handed us plates full of cake, and forks and the bluebird napkins.

"My daughter has been spending a lot of time over here," said my mom. "I hope she is...."

Mrs. Iptweet interrupted my mom, "A treasure? Yes, Mrs. Hornby, your daughter is a treasure. She is a big help to me with the garden."

"I'm glad to hear it," said my mom.

I was glad, too, to hear that I am a treasure to Mrs. Iptweet. I took a sip of papaya juice. My head filled up with the taste and smell of orangey-pink jungle fruit. We were all quiet. No one ate any cake yet.

Mrs. Iptweet smiled at my mom and said, "I understand you are a math wizard, Mrs. Hornby."

My mom said, "No, no! I'm a bookkeeper, Mrs. Iptweet. Lots of addition and subtraction, some multiplication and division. No wizardry at all."

Mrs. Iptweet said, "What made you choose your profession, Mrs. Hornby? Did you have an enthusiasm for adding and subtracting as a child?"

"Well, not really," said my mom. My mom scrunched up her eyes. "Well, yes," she said. "Um, math was always easy for me, I guess. I never really thought about it."

"What a wonderful expertise to have, Mrs. Hornby."

"I wanted a secure job I could do anywhere. That's all, Mrs. Iptweet," my mom said. "It seemed like a good idea at the time."

"I have always appreciated the importance of numbers, and the clarity they bring to the world," said Mrs. Iptweet.

Mrs. Iptweet ate a bite of cake. My mom shifted in her seat.

"Yes. Well, um, thank you, Mrs. Iptweet," said my mom.

Mrs. Iptweet said, "Prudence tells me you are also a gourmet cook."

My mom shot me a look.

She said, "Well, I'm not a gourmet cook, Mrs. Iptweet, but I do enjoy cooking."

"That is wonderful, Mrs. Hornby. Shehera.., *Prudence*, has told me about your creative cooking."

My mom turned slowly to look at me. I knew she heard the Sheherazade part of Mrs. Iptweet's words. I took a long drink of papaya juice.

My mom said, "I'm mostly a practical cook. I do try to get as many food groups into a pan as I can."

Mrs. Iptweet said, "I see you like the math of cooking, too, Mrs. Hornby."

"Well, I guess that's true, Mrs. Iptweet. I hadn't thought of it that way."

"Numbers and counting are powerful forces for good in the world," said Mrs. Iptweet.

My mom stared at Mrs. Iptweet. Then my mom put a bite of Mrs. Iptweet's coconut cake into her mouth. I watched my mom's eyes get very wide open as she chewed. She looked at the cake on her plate. Uh oh, I thought, there is a problem with the cake. Does my mom hate the taste of this cake? Maybe my mom is allergic to coconut. Maybe my mom is going to be sick and throw up all over Mrs. Iptweet's furniture. That would be so gross. I quickly ate a bite of cake in order to check out the situation. My eyes got big, too, and my ears prickled. My whole mouth and nose and head, including my brain and my neck, filled up with the taste of a creamy coconut party. My mom put another big forkful of cake into her mouth.

"Mithuth Iptweet," said my mom, "thith ith a delithuth cake."

I could hardly believe my ears and eyes, but my mom was talking with her mouth full of cake.

Coconut Cloud Cake

"Thank you, Mrs. Hornby. I am glad you like it. I wonder how many food groups are in it. I'll get the recipe and we'll count them up."

Mrs. Iptweet got up and went into her kitchen. My mom and I chomped on the best cake in the world, and washed it down with jungle fruit juice.

My mom looked around Mrs. Iptweet's living room. I noticed her eyes find the twinkle lights around the edge of the ceiling and follow the lights up the stairway. The living room hammocks are blue. The dining room hammock is striped yellow and white. My mom rubbed her hand on the fuzzy purple sofa cushions we were sitting on and picked up the doll sitting nearest to her. It was a floppy girl doll made out of cloth, with blue yarn hair and a bright yellow dress. One eye was green, the other eye was purple. A small smile came on to my mom's face. My mom took another sip of papaya juice. My mom's face looked soft. I always feel softer, too, whenever I sit for a while in Mrs. Iptweet's house and eat yum-ola food.

Mrs. Iptweet came back into the living room with a white card in her hand.

"Four. Four food groups are in this cake. How interesting. This cake was my great grandmother's recipe."

My mom looked at Mrs. Iptweet.

"You've done very interesting things with your house, Mrs. Iptweet. It's very, um, colorful. And charming."

"Thank you, Mrs. Hornby. What a nice thing to say," said Mrs. Iptweet. "Shall I give you a tour? Prudence, would you like to go and water the garden while I give your mom a spin around the house? The plants are very thirsty after the weekend."

I could tell Mrs. Iptweet wanted to be alone with my mom and talk grown-up woman talk about recipes and house decoration.

I said, "Sure, Mrs. Iptweet."

I bounced down the cellar stairs and out the back door to Mrs. Iptweet's garden. The plants grew a lot over the warm June weekend. I wondered if the plants were as glad to see me as I was to see them. I turned on the water and set the nozzle to SHOWER. I could hear my mom's and Mrs. Iptweet's voices as they walked through Mrs. Iptweet's house. When they got to the two upstairs back rooms, my mom and Mrs. Iptweet leaned out the windows and waved at me.

"Hello down there, Prudence," and "Good job, Miss Girl," they said.

I could hear bits of their words.

"Mrs. Hornby, I hope you will share with me some of your favorite mathematical recipes."

I heard my mom say, "Sure, Mrs. Iptweet."

Mrs. Iptweet said, "I think you will find this book very interesting, Mrs. Hornby."

My mom answered, "Please call me Jane, Mrs. Iptweet."

That was all I heard because then they walked to a far-from-me part of the house.

Mrs. Iptweet and my mom ended their tour at the garden. My mom could not believe how many plants and flowers and leafy things were growing in Mrs. Iptweet's patch of dirt. I showed my mom the Earth Art Creation on the driveway. Last Tuesday we made a unicorn design out of the gravel and stones. My mom was holding a book in one hand and a brown bag in the other. The title of the book read *Numerology Made Easy*. I hoped the brown bag was full of coconut cake.

My mom said, "Thank you for the loan of the book, Elizabeth, and for a lovely afternoon."

For a minute, I did not know who my mom was talking to. I looked around. It was only us three standing in the back alley at Mrs. Iptweet's house. I realized, oh, Elizabeth is Mrs. Iptweet's first name. Elizabeth Iptweet. Elizabeth is a good name for Mrs. Iptweet to have, I thought. A lot of queens are named Elizabeth.

"Jane, what a pleasure. Thank you for coming," said Mrs. Iptweet.

"Prudence, you can stay and finish up your work with Mrs. Iptweet. I'm going to make us a nice dinner." My mom held up the brown bag in her hand. "We have a special dessert tonight."

I said, "Okay, Mom. Thanks. See you in a while, Mom."

We watched my mom walk up the back alleyway.

Mrs. Iptweet turned to me and said, "We had a lovely chat, your mom and I. What a fine person she is, Prudy Gal."

I said, "Yeah. Thanks, Mrs. Iptweet."

"Your mom had a suggestion about the parade, Chérie."

I gulped.

"You talked to my mom about the parade, Mrs. Iptweet?"

"Oh, yes. I enlisted her help. We need all the help we can get because there are no notes in our Sign-up Box today, Chérie."

"Oh no, Mrs. Iptweet," I said. "What do we do now, Mrs. Iptweet?"

"Your mother had a good idea. She thinks we should have food at the parade. A table of refreshments set up on the sidewalk will help attract parade spectators, don't you think, Chérie? I have agreed to make the coconut cake." She smiled.

"Oh," I said. "Yes, food is good idea, Mrs. Iptweet. But what about getting people to march in the parade, Mrs. Iptweet?"

"And your mother has promised to provide three large bowls of something she makes that is called Divine Divinity," Mrs. Iptweet went on.

I gasped. My mom's Divine Divinity is the best food my mom makes. It is an extremely yummy food. Divine Divinity got its name because it tastes the same way that heaven tastes. Divine Divinity only has three food groups in it, but they are the three best food groups: dairy, fruit, and marshmallows.

Mrs. Iptweet said, "About inspiring our neighbors to march in the parade, Chérie, I am afraid it is time for us to take Drastic Action."

I was glad to hear this because I really like taking Drastic Action. Drastic Action is exciting and interesting.

"Great, Mrs. Iptweet," I said. "What are we going to do?"

Mrs. Iptweet stood tall in her beautiful lacy dress, purple belt, and red shoes.

"Chérie," she said. "It is time for us to go door-to-door."

CHAPTER FOURTEEN

We Take Drastic Action

"Door-to-door, Mrs. Iptweet?" I asked. "What do you mean by that exactly? Do you mean we knock on doors and talk to our neighbors? Like right at their houses? In person? Face to face?"

"That's exactly what I mean, Sheherazade," said Mrs. Iptweet.

I said, "Oh."

My mom has a strong opinion about neighbors. My mom says when it comes to neighbors, it is best to M.Y.O.B. That means Mind-Your-Own-Beeswax. M.Y.O.B. is a good way to avoid problems and aggravation. Aggravation aggravates my mom. Luckily, I don't mind aggravation that much.

The very next day, Mrs. Iptweet and I took Drastic Action for parade success.

To make an inspiring impression on our neighbors, Mrs.

Iptweet and I decided to wear mythic outfits for our door-to-door project. After school, I put on my pink butterfly blouse, my green skirt with the dragonflies all over it, my yellow socks and my extremely special red shoes from my Aunt Belle.

For my ninth birthday, Aunt Belle stuffed a birthday note and birthday money for me into the toe of a worn-out red shoe. Aunt Belle wrote my name and address onto the side of the red shoe and taped plenty of postage stamps on the high heel. Her note to me read:

Happy Birthday, Sweet-Thing Baby-Girl,
    Red shoes are good for the soul and they go with everything. Get yourself a nice pair and send me a picture.
    No dawdling.

                      Love to you,
                      Auntie Bellissima

I liked this present a lot, but my mom did not.

My mom made the tsking sound and muttered, "She does this on purpose."

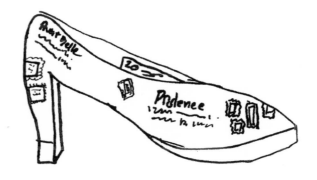

Red Shoe Postal Creation

But my mom drove me to the shoe store at the mall anyway. My mom sat in the shoe store chair next to me with her head in her hands while the shoe man brought me many pairs of red shoes to try on. On my way to the register with my new red high-top sneakers, my mom pointed to a pair of tan leather shoes.

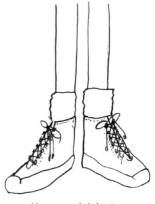

My red high-tops

She said, "What about these?"

I shook my head.

I said, "Sorry, Mom."

My red high-top sneakers are definitely my most mythic pair of shoes, so that is what I put on my feet for door-to-door day.

I met Mrs. Iptweet at her front door. Mrs. Iptweet had on a black and white stripey dress and black sequined sandals. Her hat was white straw, covered with springy black feathers.

"Are you a Mythic Zebra, Mrs. Iptweet?" I asked.

"Thank you, Zaady Gal, for noticing," said Mrs. Iptweet. "You look positively mythic yourself, Sheherazade. Great outfit."

"Hey, thanks, Mrs. Iptweet," I said. "Um, are you sure door-to-door is the best way, Mrs. Iptweet?"

I still had some nervous feelings happening inside me.

Mrs. Iptweet said, "Life presents us with many opportunities to be daring and courageous, Chérie. If we breathe deeply and hold hands we will get through it just fine."

I took a deep breath and said, "Okey dokey, Mrs. Iptweet."

I was in charge of the blue sparkle pen and the sign-up sheet on Mrs. Iptweet's special clipboard. Mrs. Iptweet painted the clipboard bright blue with yellow swirls to accentuate the Midsummer theme. We wrote a list of Mythical Creatures in case somebody needed help picking one out.

Mrs. Iptweet said, "Are we ready?"

I nodded.

"Here we go," said Mrs. Iptweet. Mrs. Iptweet took my hand in hers. We crossed the street and walked up to our first house.

Mrs. Iptweet said, "Sheherazade, we are about to have a Learning Experience. Smile."

At the first three houses we knocked and knocked, but no one came to the door. I wondered if the people were not at home, or if maybe they were hiding inside under their sofas until we went away. Is this a boring neighborhood or what, I thought.

At the fourth house, number four-o-seven, Mrs. Iptweet reached up to knock on the door like usual. But I noticed something.

I said, "Wait, Mrs. Iptweet. Look! It's an elephant."

In the middle of the door was a door knocker in the shape of an elephant's head.

Mrs. Iptweet said, "Oh, my. How right you are, Sheherazade. It's an elephant all right."

Mrs. Iptweet lifted up the trunk of the elephant-shaped door knocker and let it slam onto the door three times.

For a minute there was no sound. Then we heard the clicking sounds of a lot of locks unlocking. The dark green door opened and the tiny face of an elderly lady peeked out. The tiny lady looked us up and down.

She said, "Well? What is it?"

Mrs. Iptweet said, "Hello there, ma'am. We are the Midsummer's Day Mythical Creatures Parade Organizational Committee and we're your neighbors."

Mrs. Iptweet said our names to the lady.

"We are here to personally invite you to participate in this upcoming neighborhood festivity, guaranteed to delight and inspire you for years to come."

I said, "Yes, ma'am, it will be really fun."

The lady stared at us some more but she did not close the door. She was looking at Mrs. Iptweet's hat.

Mrs. Iptweet said, "We couldn't help but notice your interesting door knocker. I've never seen an elephant-shaped door knocker before. Wherever did it come from, I wonder?"

"Got it on my last safari, back in '39. They knew how to make a door knocker in those days. This Nairobi knocker knocks so I can hear it."

"Safari? You were on a safari?" Mrs. Iptweet asked.

The lady smiled and said, "Etta May Smithee. Call me Etta. Come on in and explain to me what the heck you're talking about."

Mrs. Iptweet said, "Why, thank you, Etta, we'd love to. What a lovely name you have, Etta."

We went inside and sat on Mrs. Smithee's leopard sofa and her tiger-striped chairs. I looked around Mrs. Smithee's living room, and everywhere I looked I saw pretend elephants. All sizes of elephants, made out of wood, stone, glass, and even seashells, were hanging around on tabletops and in bookcases and on shelves. I could tell that Mrs. Smithee liked elephants the best of all wild animals.

Mrs. Smithee told us all about her African adventures: safaris and quinine and Nairobi, and extremely large mosquitoes, and the Great Rift Valley, and Shambu. Shambu was the baby elephant who saved Mrs. Smithee's life during a wildebeest stampede.

Mrs. Smithee said, "I love all the wild animals of Africa, but the best one of all, in my mind, is the elephant."

I knew it!

After a long time of listening, Mrs. Iptweet said, "Etta, please join us in the Mythical Creatures Parade. Perhaps you'd like to honor your elephant friend who saved you."

Mrs. Smithee agreed that it was the perfect opportunity to give a special remembrance thank you to Shambu.

"It's the least I can do," said Mrs. Smithee. Tears came into Mrs. Smithee's eyes. "I haven't talked about Shambu in a long time."

Mrs. Iptweet smiled and nodded her head. Then she reached over and patted Mrs. Smithee's tiny bony hand. I wrote onto our sign-up list: Mrs. Etta May Smithee, the Mythic Elephant.

We left Mrs. Smithee's house and stood on the sidewalk. Mrs. Iptweet tapped her finger onto the midsummery clipboard.

She said, "What a wonderful success we are having, Chérie. We are making progress. Things are looking up."

"Yes, Mrs. Iptweet. Now there are three of us in the parade."

"Exactly, Chérie!"

Mrs. Iptweet walked me back to my house.

"And who knows what amazingness will come our way tomorrow on our street, Chérie? What new fascinating persons will answer the doors tomorrow afternoon? I can hardly wait," said Mrs. Iptweet.

The next day we knocked on the brown peely-paint door at number four-fifteen. A tall, skinny teenager answered the door. His hair was black and long and stringy. In one hand, he was holding a soda can. In his other hand, he held a banana with its skin half off.

He looked at us and said, "Yeah?"

I noticed he wore baggy black pants, a baggy black tee shirt, and had a big dragon tattoo on his arm.

Mrs. Iptweet explained, "Hi there, Young Man. I am Mrs. Iptweet. This is Prudence Hornby. We are your neighbors. We are putting together a Mythical Creatures parade for Midsummer's Day and we are looking for people to march in the parade."

The young man said, "Yeah. Whatever."

He started to close the door.

Mrs. Iptweet said, "That is a most amazing tattoo, Young Man. Did a local tattoo artist do that for you?"

"Um, yeah. Vinnie at Rocko's Tattoo Garden."

Mrs. Iptweet stepped closer and took hold of his arm.

"Look at the detail in this, Chérie. It's very well done."

I leaned over for a close look at the blue, red and black fire-breathing dragon.

I said, "Yeah. I can even see the scales on the dragon's tail. Wow."

The steel pin in the teenager's lip didn't seem to cause him any pain when he stretched his lips into a smile. But just looking at the steel pin made my whole face hurt.

He was feeling more friendly towards us now.

He said, "Hey. Thanks. Yeah."

"What is your name, Young Sir?" Mrs. Iptweet asked.

"Um. Zack," he said.

"Zack," said Mrs. Iptweet, "is the Dragon your animal spirit guide?"

Zack pulled his arm away from us and took a swig of soda.

"Um. I'm pretty sure it is. I think. Wait a minute," he said.

Zack yelled up the stairs, "Yo, Zelda, com'ere for a minute, would'ja?"

We heard an upstairs door open and close, then the bare feet of Zelda appeared on the stairway. Zelda walked slowly down the stairs. I knew right away that Zelda was Zack's girlfriend. I could tell they were in love by how their eyes met. Like they know and like everything about each other. Plus, Zack and Zelda have a lot in common because both their names begin with the letter Z and they both wear black clothes.

Zack said our names to Zelda, and asked Zelda if she thought his animal spirit guide was a Dragon.

Zelda looked at us and said, "Yeah, definitely."

Badly-drawn lion

Zelda had a tattoo, too. Her tattoo is a picture of a lion. A friend of hers in California did it for her when she was fourteen. Now she is seventeen. I thought it was nice of her friend to tattoo her, but her friend does not draw very well. The lion has a triangle face, and the tail is scrawny, and the claws are way too big, and one front leg of the lion is too short. This is a tattoo of a limping lion, I thought. But I did not mention my thoughts to Zelda. Zelda really likes her lion tattoo. She says she lets it show all the time. On this day she had on a black stretchy top. Her top had no back, just thin black straps that laced up and down and crisscrossed in loops, so her lion tattoo was not covered up at all. Even Zelda's long wavy brown hair was not so long that it blocked the view of the badly-drawn lion.

Zelda said, "Lions mean power and strength."

"Yes, they do," said Mrs. Iptweet. "Power and strength are good things for a young woman to have, Zelda."

Zelda said, "Rock on, Mrs. Ip."

I told Zack and Zelda all the parade details. Then I said, "There's going to be food, too."

Zack and Zelda said, "Cool."

I wrote down Zelda and Zack on the Parade Participants list: Zack, the Mythic Dragon, and Zelda, the Queen of Beasts.

At number four-twenty-two, it was my turn to do the talking. Mrs. Iptweet stood behind me. I lifted my hand to knock on the dark blue door, but my hand just knocked on air because the door swung wide open very fast.

"Hey, what's happening? Who are you two? I've been watching you for days. You've been to a lot of houses and finally you are here. You're not religious fanatics are you? I already have a religion."

The lady had short, curly white hair, and a fast way of talking through her big smile.

I said, "Greetings, Neighbor. We're the Parade Organizing Committee here to speak to you about signing up to be in our Midsummer's Day Parade. What's your favorite Mythical Creature, ma'am?"

Then I remembered to say our names, too.

"Right," said the lady. "I saw the signs and flyers. Great graphics. Loved them, seriously. But I thought it was a joke. Hah! What do you mean Mythical Creatures? What are you talking about? Come on in, this is gonna take a while, I can tell. I'm Katie Van Rooken. Lived here thirty years, you gals must be newer."

Mrs. Van Rooken kept on talking to us all the way into her house, through her blue living room, past her blue dining room, and into her blue kitchen.

She said, "Sit yourselves down right here. How about some orange juice? Everybody loves orange juice and it's good for you, too. Gives you an energy boost. Kept me going at the swim meets. Oranges are full of energy. That's because they grow in hot places in bright sunlight. I can see you two need an energy boost right now. You have a lot of explaining to do, now don't you. Sit yourselves down already, will ya?"

She poured orange juice into three huge green glasses and sat down at the kitchen table with Mrs. Iptweet and me. She put her elbows on the table; her hands held her chin.

She said, "Okay, let's hear it."

Mrs. Iptweet drank her juice and winked at me. It was still my turn to do the talking.

I said, "Thanks very much, Mrs. Van..."

Mrs. Van Rooken interrupted me, "That's good. Call me Mrs. Van. It's easier to say and spell. Should have thought of it years ago. I believe in keeping things simple and straightforward – it serves one well in life. I have found that out the hard way, of course."

I said, "Okay, Mrs. Van."

I looked around Mrs. Van's kitchen. Right away, I noticed Mrs. Van's refrigerator because it had about one hundred magnets stuck onto it. All the magnets were in the shapes of different kinds of fishes.

"I never saw so many fish magnets in one place, Mrs. Van," I said, "You are really into fish and magnetism, huh, Mrs. Van."

"Hah! Yeah! It was my nickname. Miss Fish. They called me Miss Fish way back when I was a swimmer."

Mrs. Iptweet and I looked at each other. Our eyes were wide open because we were both surprised and shocked to hear about Mrs. Van's nickname.

"Championship swimmer. Golly gee, I loved to swim and feel the water holding me up and me moving through it so smooth and fast. Broke records at the regional level. Used to imagine I was a barracuda when I raced. Who could beat a barracuda in a swimming pool, I ask you?"

"Probably no regular people, Mrs. Van," I said.

I added her name to the list.

That night, I wrote my news to Aunt Belle.

Dear Aunt Belle,
    Our Midsummer's Day Mythical Creatures
Parade is coming along pretty good. Mrs. Van will be the
Mythic Mermaid, even though her hair is short. Soon I
have to make my Mythic Storyteller costume. I do not
have any Arabian or Persian clothes, but Mrs. Iptweet
has sequins and a glue gun. I wish you could be in our
parade.

                              Love, Your Niece,
                                 Prudence

CHAPTER FIFTEEN

Knock, Knock

At the end of two afternoons of going door-to-door, we had three Not-At-Home's, eleven I-Don't-Think-So's, one Come-Back-Later, and four parade participants. Mrs. Iptweet and I celebrated our door-to-door success at her studio.

Mrs. Iptweet said, "Chérie, let's see. So far a Dragon, a Mythic Elephant, the Queen of Beasts, and a Mermaid. Oh, the Amazingness of Life, Chérie."

"Yeah. Um. That makes six people in the parade, Mrs. Iptweet."

"It will be a small and charming parade, Chérie. And we've only been to nineteen houses. Who knows what will happen or who we will meet at the last eleven houses tomorrow?"

We drank glasses of apple juice and ate cut-up apples.

"Apples are a part of so many ancient stories from olden times, Chéri," Mrs. Iptweet said. "Apples are a Mythic Fruit, it seems."

I said, "Yeah, Mrs. Iptweet."

I drank three glasses of the Mythic Juice. Knocking on doors, writing lists, and talking to neighbors made me extremely thirsty.

"Tomorrow, same time, Chérie?"

"Okey dokey, Mrs. Iptweet," I said.

That night I stayed up late, until 9:30 p.m., in my Dream-o-rama. I wrote my last essay for fourth grade homework. Miss McKelvey, my fourth grade teacher, believes in learning up until the last minute.

When I finished my essay, I put my blue ink pen away and cuddled up under my bedspread in my Dream-o-rama. I had a lot of thoughts while I was falling into sleepiness. Who else will be in our parade, I wondered? Maybe someone will want to be a unicorn. That would be so interesting. How is Mrs. Smithee going to make herself look like an elephant? What am I going to wear for a Mythic Storyteller costume? None of my clothes are sparkly or spangly. Sheherazade of Arabia always wore shiny, sparkly fancy clothes even when she was relaxing. What would she have worn in a parade?

When I woke up in the morning, I still did not know the answers to my questions, so I got dressed and went to school. First thing after the bell rang, it was time to read our "What am I Planning to Do on My Summer Vacation" essays. Billy Hanrahan read his essay first. He is going to visit his Uncle Jimbo in Wisconsin and learn how to fish in a lake. Charmaine Greeley told our class she is going to the seashore for the whole summer. Charmaine will play on the beach, eat water ice, and help her mom take care of their newborn baby, Oscar.

It was my turn next. I walked to the front of the class.

I read my title first, "My Summer Vacation, Fun or Disaster? You Decide."

"The first thing I am doing on my summer vacation is making a parade. It is called the Midsummer's Day Mythical Creatures Parade. So far there are six people, total, in the parade. Maybe there will be more after today, I am not sure yet. Anything could happen."

"I am not making this parade all by myself. I have a new friend since March. She is a grown-up, but I do not mind. Her name is Mrs. Iptweet, for real, and she lives on my street. My street used to be boring, but even though it is the same street as before, now it is not boring anymore."

"In only ten days, we are having the parade. It takes a lot of time to make a parade because you cannot buy a parade in a catalog. You have to make it yourself. Usually your friends and neighbors, and maybe your family, are in the parade with you. This parade is happening on a very important day called the Summer Solstice. It is marked on your calendars. You can look it up."

"I think Mythical Creatures are very interesting and mythic. Mythical Creatures, like dragons and mermaids, help human beings with living on earth by inspiring them to be brave and to do interesting things."

"Even though we only have six people signed up to march in the parade, including me and Mrs. Iptweet, and it might be a disaster, Mrs. Iptweet says we will have fun no matter what and that charm counts for a lot and that some nuts are hard to crack. After the parade is done, I will go to summer camp at our neighborhood camp because my mom works. That's it. The end."

Everybody just sat there when I was done. I thought, maybe they think there is more.

I said, "That's it, the end," again, so everyone would know for sure my essay was over. My friend Bea Bea started to clap and everyone else joined in.

Ms. McKelvey said, "Thank you, Prudence. My, what an interesting way to start the summer."

I said, "Thank you, Ms. McKelvey."

I walked back to my seat. Ms. McKelvey held her chin in her hand for a while.

"Yes, very interesting," she said again.

That afternoon after lunch, my whole class got a very big surprise. Ms. McKelvey canceled our regular Thursday math lesson and made the Mythical Creatures Parade our lesson.

She said, "Oh, it's almost summer, let's have some fun."

Everybody in my class was happy about this except Johnny Wesbacker, who likes math.

We had a big discussion about parades and imaginary animals and the sun in the sky. Ms. McKelvey used her special box of colored chalk to write a list of our favorite Pretend Animals and Creatures onto the blackboard. Some of my classmates even asked me if they could be in the parade, too.

After school, I went to Mrs. Iptweet's house with a list in my pocket. When I got there, I saw that Mrs. Iptweet was making adjustments to her reindeer hat. She pulled on the antlers to get them to stand up straighter, but still the fuzzy antlers flopped to the sides. This was because the antlers were made out of stuffed material.

Mrs. Iptweet muttered, "I need some wire."

Mrs. Iptweet walked to the far side of the studio. She used her wire clipping tool to clip two pieces of heavy wire off of her roll of steely strong wire.

I called after her, "Hey, Mrs. Iptweet, guess what? Some kids from my class at school want to be in our parade. I told them I would have to check with you during our parade organizing committee meeting first."

"That is tremendous good news, Chérie!" Mrs. Iptweet said.

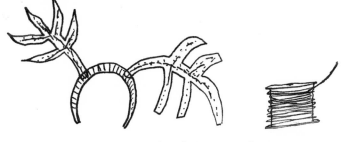

Antler hat and wire

"Let's call this meeting to order right now."

Mrs. Iptweet took off her antler hat and stuck the pieces of wire into the cloth antlers.

"I vote yes. Let's let your classmates participate. What do you vote?"

Mrs. Iptweet passed me some crackers and cheese and a glass of chocolate milk.

"It's okay with me, Mrs. Iptweet," I said. "I vote yes."

I chomped on a crunchy cracker and a piece of tangy cheese while Mrs. Iptweet put the Rudolph hat back on her head. The antlers stood up pretty straight now.

I wrote in a special category on our Parade Participants list: The Fourth Graders. I will tell my fourth grade friends the good news tomorrow about their being accepted into the Mythical Creatures parade.

I took a long drink of chocolate milk, and Mrs. Iptweet and I started out to visit the last houses on our street.

We had more Not-At-Homes and No-Thanks houses all the way to the end of our street. At the corner, I figured it was time to turn around and go to our very last house. But Mrs. Iptweet didn't turn around to walk back down Durham Street. Mrs. Iptweet pointed to a house across the way, on the side street, a house with a red door.

Mrs. Iptweet said, "That is where Yolanda lives."

Mrs. Iptweet looked at me and smiled and raised her eyebrows.

"I think you will like Yolanda, Chérie."

We walked across the street and Mrs. Iptweet pushed the doorbell button.

She called out, "Good Afternoon, Yolanda. It's me, Elizabeth."

The big red door opened. In the doorway stood Yolanda. Yolanda filled up the whole space of the doorway. Yolanda was tall and wide. She had on shorts and a tee shirt, so I could see a lot of her dark blue-black skin.

"Hi there, Liz. Great to see you. Come on in," said Yolanda.

We stepped into Yolanda's house.

"Thank you, Yolanda. Prudence, meet our neighbor, Yolanda Ngoren. Let me introduce my Lovely Assistant, Yolanda. This is Prudence Hornby," said Mrs. Iptweet.

Yolanda said, "Nice to meet you, Prudence. Call me Yolanda."

I said, "Hi, Yolanda. Nice to meet you, too."

Yolanda sat down on her sofa, and flipped her hair back. Yolanda's long hair made a lot of clacking and clicking noises because of all the beads braided into it. Yolanda had about one thousand braids in her hair, all over her head.

Yolanda's hair, full of beads

"Sit down over here, Prudy. I wanna hear more about this project you two got going."

I sat down next to Yolanda and looked around her living

room. Pretty much everything was red. The walls, the sofa and chairs, and the rug. Everything except for the gold mirror wall and the drums. The drums were black and white and shiny. I told Yolanda about our parade idea, and about Mythical Creatures and imaginary animals.

"Cool," said Yolanda. "I can do that. But I don't wanna be no animal. I wanna be Goddess of the Nile. I have got me a great goddess outfit."

Mrs. Iptweet turned to me.

"Shall we bend the rules in this case, Chérie, about Mythical Creatures?"

I said, "Sure, Mrs. Iptweet."

I wrote Yolanda's name onto the Parade Participants list: Yolanda Ngoren, Goddess of the Nile.

Then Yolanda told me about her life as a drummer. I told Yolanda about my dad and his banjo.

Yolanda said, "Huh. Banjo."

After our visit with Yolanda, Mrs. Iptweet and I made our very last stop. We went to see Mrs. Romero at number four-o-two. Mrs. Romero remembered me from the day her parakeet escaped for a few minutes last summer.

"Oh, was that not a terrible day, Little One?" Mrs. Romero put her hand over her heart. "The day I almost lost La Señora!"

Mrs. Romero crossed herself and invited us in to say hello to Señora Puff o' Fluff.

Señora Puff o' Fluff's birdcage sits right on the coffee table in front of Mrs. Romero's tan sofa.

I leaned over and whispered, "Hi, Bird."

Señora Puff o' Fluff hopped from one perching stick to another and looked at me with one of her tiny eyes.

I did a good job of introducing Mrs. Iptweet to Mrs. Romero. Mrs. Iptweet and I told Mrs. Romero all about the parade.

"Do you have a favorite Mythical Creature, Mrs. Romero?" I asked.

Mrs. Romero covered her mouth and laughed. "No, no, no, not me, Little One. I am too shy to march in a parade."

Mrs. Romero opened up the door to the white metal parakeet cage, and the little green bird hopped out, right onto Mrs. Romero's finger.

"But La Señora is not shy at all. La Señora, she loves parades."

Mrs. Romero lifted her finger full of green fluff over to my shoulder. Señora Puff o' Fluff hopped onto me and made a tiny bird tweeting sound into my ear.

"I can see she is not a shy bird, Mrs. Romero," said Mrs. Iptweet. "Perhaps Señora Puff o' Fluff could portray a Mythic Parakeet in the parade."

Tweet tweet

"That is a great idea, Mrs. Iptweet! Yes, Señora? Are we agreed? I will dress you up as the mythic bird of my ancestors in ancient Mexico."

Mrs. Romero put out her finger and Señora Puff o' Fluff hopped off my shoulder.

"Quetzalcoatl, yes?"

La Señora made some happy-sounding twitters. This means we will have a Real Live Creature portraying a Mythical Creature in our parade.

That night I wrote a letter to my Aunt Belle.

Dear Aunt Belle,

The parade has eleven people in it now. Way better than two people. My mom says this Saturday we will buy a lot of fruit, milk and marshmallows. We are making enough Divine Divinity to feed the neighborhood. How are you?

How is Bessie the Wonder Horse?

Love, Your Niece,
Prudy

CHAPTER SIXTEEN

I Crack the Code

The next day was gray and rainy. The gloomy drizzle did not make me feel gloomy or drizzly though. I headed to my last day of fourth grade with a smile on my face. My yellow slicker and fisherman hat kept me dry for the six-block walk to my school.

My teacher, Ms. McKelvey, did special activities for our last day. We took turns reading from Ms. McKelvey's favorite story book. Then Ms. McKelvey gave us a special memento to remember her by: a reading list for summer. We had a big discussion about reading every week and not letting our brains rot just because the weather was hot.

Ms. McKelvey asked me if I had any news about my parade.

I stood up and used my loud announcement voice, "Everyone is invited to be a Mythical Creature in the Durham Street Parade."

My classmates clapped. Ms. McKelvey used her blue chalk to write the important parade details about when and where to meet onto the blackboard. I noticed a lot of my classmates copied the words into their notebooks.

Ms. McKelvey asked, "Are we all invited to watch the parade, too, Prudence?"

I blinked and said, "Yes, sure, Ms. McKelvey."

"We will now do a lesson on Preparedness, Class," said Ms. McKelvey. "If a person goes to watch a parade, what would be important to bring?"

So the last thing we learned in fourth grade was about lawn chairs and coolers.

On my way home from my last day of fourth grade forever, I walked slowly through the raindrops and I had a lot of thoughts. What will fifth grade be like? Will my classmates really show up at the parade? Will Ms. McKelvey come to watch the parade? What am I going to do about my Mythic Storyteller costume? Maybe I will go to Mrs. Iptweet's house today and ask for parade outfit advice. Maybe Mrs. Iptweet studied costumes at her great school, too.

I got home pretty fast and I walked up my front steps. At the top step, I had to stop. My porch was blockaded by an old suitcase. Why is this suitcase on my porch, I wondered? It was an old-fashioned suitcase, green leather, kind of small, and no wheels on the bottom.

I called out, "Hey, Mom, are you taking a nap? Hey, wake up, Mom. Mom, whose suitcase is this? Who is here for a visit, Mom?"

I looked at the other side of the suitcase. On that side, I saw a label pasted right in the middle and postage stamps pasted in the upper corner. I climbed over the suitcase, out of the rain, and leaned in close to read the writing on the label. The writing was my name and address. I gasped out loud. I gasped so loud, my mom heard me.

She called out the front door with her sleepy voice, "Prudy, are you all right?"

I yelled, "Mom, this suitcase is addressed to me! Mom, this suitcase is a letter!"

My mind and my whole body were full of excitement. My arms flapped around, and my legs jumped up and down. There was only one person in the entire world who would make a suitcase into an envelope.

I shouted, "Mom, this suitcase must be from Aunt Belle, Mom. I think it's a gigantic Postal Creation. Can you believe it, Mom?" A big laugh came out of me. "I'm going to open it now, Mom. Okay?"

My mom came outside onto the porch. She was rubbing the beauty sleep out of her eyes.

"What has she come up with now?" asked my mom.

I carried the suitcase to the porch sofa and my mom and I sat down with the Postal Creation between us. My mom helped me pop open the suitcase clasps. I lifted the lid. A gigantic mound of orange tissue paper billowed out. I pulled out the tissue paper and I gasped loudly again. Some kind of a bright sparkly golden thing was snuggled into the orange paper. I lifted the something up. It was light and soft in my hand. It was a dress, a golden dress. It was the most beautiful dress I ever saw that was my size.

Gold lamé
power dress

My mom said, "Good grief, it's gold lamé." Then she put her head in her hands.

I said, "I like gold lamé, Mom. Gold lamé is great."

I saw a note pinned onto the fancy

dress. I unpinned and unfolded the secret dress note and read it out loud so my mom could hear, too.

Howdy Sherry Zadee, Sweet Thing Baby Girl,
   Your secret power name suits you well. When a girl gets a power name, it's only a minute more till she gets a power outfit. Sorry I can't be there to march with you, Darlin'. I have sent you a Mythical Creature to wear - Bessie the Wonder Horse dressed up as Pegasus, that Greek horse with wings. I want a picture.
                    Love to you, Baby Girl,
                    Aunt Bellissima

My mom was shaking her head and muttering, "I can't believe her."

I rooted around in the tissue paper until I found a small purple box. Yep, inside the box was a tiny Bessie the Wonder Horse, made out of rusty metal. In real life, Bessie is the same color as rust, so the trash art looked exactly like her. Aunt Belle glued on white tin wings and a safety pin on the back. It was a Mythical Recycled Trash Art Jewelry pin!

Bessie/Pegasus

My mom took the trash art pin into her hands and inspected it. My mom had a frowny look on her face.

"Mom, this pin looks extremely clean to me, Mom," I said. "I bet Aunt Belle scrubbed it really good, probably even with strong bleach."

I leaned over and sniffed the art.

"Yeah, Mom. It definitely smells bleachy to me." I coughed.

My mom held rusty Bessie up to her nose and breathed in.

My mom said, "Oh, all right."

She handed the mythical pin to me.

"At least you are up-to-date on your shots."

I said, "Right, Mom. Nothing to worry about at all."

I put the Mythical Bessie pin back into its box and nestled the box into the orange tissue paper next to the gold lamé Power Dress. I clicked the two clasps shut and held the suitcase by its handle. The suitcase was not too big, or too small, or too heavy.

I said to myself, "This suitcase is just my size."

My mom said, "Don't be too long at Mrs. Iptweet's today, Prudy. I'm making us an early dinner and we have to make our shopping list for tomorrow."

"Okay, Mom," I said. "I'd better get over there right now. I know Mrs. Iptweet will be amazed to see this new Postal Creation. See you later, Mom."

I gave my mom a kiss on her cheek. I skipped down our steps and ran to Mrs. Iptweet's back door fast, so I would not get my Postal Creation too wet in the rain.

I knocked hard and yelled, "Hey, Mrs. Iptweet, have I got a surprise for you."

I heard the sound of Mrs. Iptweet's voice from far inside the house.

"I'll be there in a moment, Zaady Gal."

While I waited for Mrs. Iptweet, I looked at the garden. It was thick with leaves and flowers. Feathery cosmos. Thick scratchy pumpkin vines. The Swiss chard was as high as my knees. Three red poppies were opened up. I told the plants how great they were doing.

Then I noticed something new in the garden. Right in the middle of the growing plants was a pink plastic bowl. The bowl was full of water. I heard Mrs. Iptweet's studio door swing open.

"Hello, Chérie. So sorry to keep you waiting. I was adjusting my wings. Please come in out of the wet."

"Hi, Mrs. Iptweet. Thanks, Mrs. Iptweet. Your wings look really nice," I said. "You will be a great Dove of Peace."

I went inside carrying my amazing Postal Creation.

"Wait until you see this, Mrs. Iptweet. You are not going to believe it, but it is true."

Mrs. Iptweet was amazed and shocked when I showed her Aunt Belle's Postal Creation suitcase art, my gold power dress, and the Mythical Trash Art Pegasus pin.

Mrs. Iptweet said, "Oh, the Amazingness of Life," and "I must meet your Aunt Belle someday," and "How inspirational, Chérie," and "It's the perfect dress for the Mythic Storyteller to wear in the parade. Yes, it is."

I was glad Mrs. Iptweet liked everything, but I needed more parade outfit advice.

"What about shoes, Mrs. Iptweet?" I asked. "None of my shoes are gold or sparkly."

"That's easy enough to fix, Chérie."

Mrs. Iptweet picked up her glue gun and rattled her box of sequins.

"You've got those high-top sneakers that are so nice. And they are red," said Mrs. Iptweet.

I scratched my head. "Red high-tops with gold lamé, Mrs. Iptweet?"

"Red shoes go with everything, Chérie."

"That's what my Aunt Belle says, Mrs. Iptweet. The high-tops are my most mythic shoes, I think, Mrs. Iptweet."

Mrs. Iptweet rooted through her box and found a bag of tiny bright red disks.

"We could glue red sequins onto your sneakers if you'd like more sparkle."

I nodded my head.

I said, "That sounds good to me, Mrs. Iptweet."

I sat down in the blue stripey chair, all relaxed about my parade costume. That's when I noticed Mrs. Iptweet's studio table. The table was covered with little bottles and jars. Each little jar and bottle had some kind of clear watery liquid in it. And each little bottle and jar had a paper tag tied onto it.

I also noticed that the big blue mermaid trunk was on the floor of the studio, wide open. It was the trunk I saw on the first day Mrs. Iptweet moved in to the neighborhood, the trunk inscribed with the secret code, H-2-0. Oh, wow, I thought, I am going to crack the secret code any minute now. I stood up so I would be ready.

"I thought today was a good day to add to my Water Collection, Chérie," said Mrs. Iptweet.

Mrs. Iptweet held a small empty jar in her hand.

"Would you mind bringing in the bowl of rain, Zaady Gal?"

"Your Water Collection, Mrs. Iptweet?" I asked.

It turns out that H-2-O is the secret scientific formula code name for plain old water.

I carefully carried the pink bowl full of H-2-O into the studio and watched while Mrs. Iptweet poured the wild water straight from the sky into the empty jar. Mrs. Iptweet let me write the label with her sky blue sparkle pen.

The bowl of rain

I wrote "Midsummer Rain, Durham Street."

We placed the jar of rain next to the other jars full of wild water on the table. I read some of the tags: Atlantic Ocean, Pacific Ocean, Bay of Fundy, Hot Springs near Swan Lake, Mississippi River, Hailstorm 1984, First Snow 1993, and Cow Creek.

Mrs. Iptweet said, "I carry a small glass jar in my purse in case I come across an interesting stream, pond, lake, rivulet or ocean. It's good to be prepared, I find, Chérie."

"Why do you collect water, Mrs. Iptweet?" I asked.

"It makes you think, doesn't it, Chérie?"

"Yes, I guess so, Mrs. Iptweet."

I was thinking about all the different places in the world, and where does water come from, and why would anybody give water a secret code name.

That night I wrote to my Aunt Belle.

Dear Aunt Belle,

I love gold lamé. I will wear the Mythic Flying Horse pin for sure. I cracked a secret code by accident today, and I thought about the meaning of water on purpose. How are you?

Love from me,
Sheherazade Hornby, your Niece

CHAPTER SEVENTEEN

Parade Day

Our neighborhood paraders came every afternoon to Mrs. Iptweet's studio. We did a lot of gluing, taping, sewing and pinning. Sequins, feathers and cardboard come in really handy when getting ready for a parade. We attached all kinds of interesting mythic things onto hats, dresses, shirts, capes, and antlers. We made two banners and three flags.

My dad tried to call me from his new cell phone a bunch of times. I knew it was my dad because I always heard his voice say, "Honeybun..." before the scritchy-scratchy sounds and the dings and beeps drowned out his voice. I am glad my dad tried to call me, but I still do not know if my dad will be coming to play his banjo at our parade.

After dinner, on the night before the parade, my mom helped me lay out my Mythic Storyteller costume: gold lamé dress, yellow socks, red high-tops with sequins, and Aunt Belle's Trash Art Pegasus pin.

I said, "Thanks, Mom."

My mom said, "You're welcome, Darling Girl. You are all set."

Then my mom said, "Time for bed, Prudy."

I said, "Mom, it's only eight o'clock p.m. It's still light out, Mom."

"That's okay, Miss Girl. You have a big day tomorrow."

"Mom, I can't sleep while the sun is still up, Mom," I argued.

"Yes, you can, Prudy," said my mom. "I'm pulling down the shade. It's important that you get plenty of rest tonight."

"Mom," I said, "I'll be fine. It's a small parade, Mom. I'm not sleepy, Mom."

But my mom would not listen, so I climbed into my Dream-o-rama. My mom tucked in the covers all around me and kissed me on my forehead.

"Go to sleep. No fooling around," she said.

After my mom went downstairs, I turned sideways in my Dream-o-rama so I could see my Mythic Storyteller outfit on the floor. In only a few more hours I would wear it in the Midsummer's Day Parade. I decided to stay up all night and wait for the longest day of the year to arrive.

I guess I fell asleep, because the next thing I knew, I woke up. I climbed out of my Dream-o-rama and I lifted up the shade on my bedroom window. It was still dark dark night out there. I picked up my little clock off my bureau and looked at the time with my bleary sleepy eyes: 4:37 a.m. Uh oh, I thought, only three and a half more hours till our Mythical Creatures Midsummer's Day Parade starts. Time to put on my costume!

I stumbled over to my Mythic Storyteller outfit. There it

was, all glimmery and beautiful. I pulled off my pink pajamas and threw them onto my Dream-o-rama. I pulled the amazing dress on over my head. It felt soft on the inside and soft on the outside. I put on my mythic yellow socks and my high-tops. I pinned on my excellent Pegasus Trash Art pin.

I looked great, except for my hair. I searched around for my hairbrush. I found it on the floor of my closet, right next to the big white hatbox full of Gran's hat. I brushed my hair till most of the knots were out of it. My hair reaches almost to my shoulders now.

I spun around. The golden dress twirled and swirled like a ball gown. I was almost ready. I needed one more thing. I opened up the big white hatbox. There was Gran's hat waiting for me. I lifted it out and put it on my head. The tee shirt and pillowcase stuffing was still in the top, so it fit me perfectly. I looked in the mirror. Great! I wished myself good luck.

I carefully tiptoed down the stairs, and quietly unlocked our front door. I pulled the door open very slowly so it would not make the big whooshing sound, and stepped into the cool night air on our porch. I sat on the porch sofa to wait for daytime to happen. It was quiet in the dark. No footsteps, no voices, no sounds. Only once did I hear a car driving on the busy road. I laid down on the porch sofa and pulled Gran's afghan over me. I saw some twinkly stars in the sky and wondered what their names were. I listened to the big quietness. The only sound I could hear was my own heart beating.

After a while of looking and listening and thinking in the quiet darkness, I heard a twitter. I heard tweets, chirps and cheeping. The birds were waking up. I saw a small brightness at one end of the sky.

Mrs. Iptweet had told me, "The very first sign that night is

First Light

over and the day has begun is called First Light. It is very slight. You must look carefully, Chérie."

I sat up on the porch sofa and looked carefully. Yep, there it was. First Light. Each moment the brightness was a tiny bit brighter. The stars faded away. Here it is, I thought, the day I've been waiting for. The longest day of the year has begun. The day of the very first Durham Street Midsummer's Day Mythical Creatures Parade. The day I will walk down my street in a gold dress with other people pretending to be pretend animals. Yikes! Oh, no, what was I thinking? How can I be in a parade?

The First Light of Midsummer's Day came and so did the butterflies, the butterflies of extreme nervousness and excitement. First, the butterflies invaded my belly. Big flapping wings in my stomach area caused me to almost throw up. Second, my brain had a terrible dizziness and I almost fainted. Next, the winged things went into my veins, arteries and skin. This caused beads of sweat to form on me all over and a great jumpiness in my arms and legs. I had to dance around on the porch and fling my arms about.

I heard footsteps coming fast down our stairway in the house and across the living room floor and there was my mom standing in our doorway.

"What are you doing up so early? Why are you outside in the dark?" said my mom.

I kept flapping and jumping around.

I said, "Mom, it is not completely dark anymore. It's First Light, Mom. It's Midsummer's Day. I'm having a little nervousness about the parade, Mom, but I can handle it, Mom."

"I told you it was a big day," said my mom.

My mom noticed Gran's hat on the porch sofa. Mom looked at me.

I said, "I'll be careful with it, Mom."

My mom made me hot milk and toast with butter and cinnamon on it. I was so excited and filled with butterflies, only three bites of cinnamon toast fit into my stomach.

"Thanks, Mom," I said. I looked out the kitchen window. "Uh oh, Mom, the sun is up. There is a lot of light in the sky, Mom. I gotta go. Bye, Mom."

I hopped through the dining room.

"I'm going to start making the Divine Divinity now, Prudy. Then I'll set out some lawn chairs."

I was running out the front door.

"Come back here for a second."

I said, "Mom. What, Mom?"

I ran back to the kitchen and my mom hugged me.

She said, "This is your first parade. Take it easy. I'll be watching."

"Okay, Mom. Thanks, Mom."

I kissed my mom on her cheek. Then I ran out of our

house, grabbed Gran's hat and headed down the back alley to Mrs. Iptweet's.

"Hi, Mrs. Iptweet," I yelled. "The sun is definitely up now, Mrs. Iptweet."

Mrs. Iptweet's studio door swung open.

"You are right about that, Chérie."

Mrs. Iptweet was smiling a big smile. She stepped outside to join me in the early light of Midsummer's Day.

"Mrs. Iptweet, I really really like your Dove of Peace costume," I said.

She lifted her arms and spread her wings. Mrs. Iptweet looked like a soft white bird in all that white lace and feathers and white sheet material.

"Thank you, Chérie," said Mrs. Iptweet. "Chérie, you are a Mythic Vision today yourself. How beautiful you look and how lovely for you to wear your Gran's hat."

Mrs. Iptweet in her Dove of Peace costume

"Thanks, Mrs. Iptweet."

I jumped around, and my arms flapped. I couldn't help it.

"Butterflies, Zaady Gal?" asked Mrs. Iptweet.

I nodded my head.

"Yes, Mrs. Iptweet. Lots of them. I almost threw up at dawn."

Mrs. Iptweet said, "Butterflies do feel odd at first. Breathe deeply, Sheherazade. Butterflies like a lot of air."

I breathed in about a bucketful of air. Mrs. Iptweet put her hand on my back.

"Stand at your full height, Chérie. Shoulders down. Breathe right into your belly. That's it. Good job."

I felt more calm. I didn't need to bounce as high as before.

"Congratulations on being in your first parade, Sheherazade."

"Thanks, Mrs. Iptweet," I said. "Nobody is here yet, though, Mrs. Iptweet, except us."

"That is true, Chérie. Let's get out the band instruments before the rush."

We went inside and found the basket of kazoos.

"Mrs. Iptweet, do you think there will be a rush?"

My words got interrupted though. I heard the sound of running feet outside on the driveway. I scooted to the doorway of the studio and saw a gigantic bee running towards me. Stripes of crinkly black and yellow paper were wrapped all over the arms, legs, body, neck, and head of the Giant Bee. Only the eyes and nose stuck out and there was a silver tiara on the bee's head. The bee said, "Hey Prudy, it's me, Bea Bea! I'm the Mythic Queen Bee."

My friend, Bea Bea the Bee, and I hugged and jumped up and down together.

The Queen Bee

"My mom is at your house visiting your mom, Prudy. She brought popcorn and a lawn chair," said Bea Bea.

"That's great, Bea Bea," I said.

I looked over Bea Bea's shoulder and my eyes got all wide open.

"Mrs. Iptweet," I yelled in my loud voice. "Mrs. Iptweet, um, Mythical Creatures are walking down the alleyway, Mrs. Iptweet."

Mrs. Iptweet stood outside her studio door with her hands on her hips, laughing and smiling.

Mrs. Iptweet said, "Chérie, I think we are having a parade today."

I handed out the band instruments to each person as they arrived. Mostly everyone knew how to play a kazoo. I only had to show Joey, the Early Bird, how to hum into it.

Mrs. Iptweet greeted everyone and passed out apricot muffins and paper cups full of mint tea.

"Welcome, Etta," she said to Mrs. Smithee. "So nice to see you. Shambu would be proud."

Mrs. Smithee,
Mythic Elephant

Mrs. Smithee wore a plain gray dress and gray gloves, and pretended one of her arms was her Mythic Elephant trunk.

"Zelda, that's a great top. It shows off your tattoo very well."

"Hi, Zack. Have a muffin."

"Welcome, Fourth Graders. You all look wonderful!" said Mrs. Iptweet.

"Do I look mermaidy enough?" Mrs. Van called down the alley. "I am not sure about this get-up. What do you think?"

"Yes, very mermaidy, Mrs. Van," called Mrs. Iptweet.

Mrs. Van smoothed her long blue dress, pulled her white bathing cap farther down over her hair and felt her seashell necklace around her neck.

The Mythic
Mermaid

"Well, if you say so. I wish I had some seaweed or something."

"Hey, Girls, you ready for me?" I heard a loud voice say. "I told you, Liz, I had a great goddess outfit, didn't I? I bet you didn't know a goddess who played the bongo drums before, now did you?"

"You are right about that, Yolanda," said Mrs. Iptweet. "Please have a muffin."

The back alleyway was full of Mythical Creatures eating apricot muffins and drinking mint tea. Mrs. Iptweet leaned over to me.

"Everyone is here, Chérie. Let's start the parade in a little while when everyone has finished eating."

I had a giggly feeling inside me and I had a sad feeling, too. Everyone is here except for my dad, I thought.

"Mrs. Iptweet, what about my dad? He isn't here yet."

"Sheherazade, is your dad coming to the parade? How wonderful!"

"Um, Mrs. Iptweet, I don't know exactly for sure if he will be here. But definitely maybe."

Mrs. Iptweet put her wings around me.

"We can wait a few more minutes, Sheherazade. Let's wait a few more minutes."

Then she called out to our group of paraders, "When you are finishing chewing, Everyone, let's practice kazooing our parade theme song, *You Are My Sunshine*."

I walked down the alleyway to the busy street to keep a lookout for my dad. It is a short distance to the busy street from Mrs. Iptweet's house. I looked both ways, up and down the street, in search of my dad on his motorcycle. Just a lot of dumb old ordinary cars were driving by. I closed my eyes. I listened for the grumbly, rumbly sound of my dad's motorcycle. I tried to let the hearing power of my ears stretch to hear all the sounds from far away. Lots of city noises were happening, but no motorcycles.

Across the street, I noticed that Big Nick and Little Nick, the owners of the Corner Market, were opening their store for the day. Little Nick had a stack of newspapers in his arms. Little Nick probably had a big day planned, full of coupon-cutting crimes to commit. I remembered when watching the Nicks commit crimes was interesting to me, back in the days when my life was boring.

I checked the street and listened for motorcycle sounds again. No luck. Probably my dad had some big important playing gig to do. Usually my dad marches for miles playing his banjo in long, important, professional parades. It is small potatoes for my dad to play in a one-street parade. Probably he was trying to tell me all about his other work when he called the other day. Probably his cell phone didn't work very well because he is far away doing something extremely important. I turned and walked the short way back to the gathering of parade participants.

Mrs. Iptweet was introducing everybody to each other.

"Let's welcome our Mythic Mermaid for today, Mrs. Van Rooken," said Mrs. Iptweet.

Mrs. Van waved at everybody. Everybody clapped for Mrs. Van.

She said, "I wish I had some seaweed."

I thought Mrs. Van's long blue dress looked good, and even though Mrs. Van does not have long wavy mermaid hair, her short white curls looked nice sticking out from under her bathing cap.

Mrs. Iptweet said, "Katherine, your basket full of clam chowder soup cans is the perfect touch."

"Now, Everyone, meet our Mythic Elephant, Mrs. Etta Smithee. Etta, you are a vision in gray today."

We clapped for Mrs. Smithee. Mrs. Smithee is even shorter

than a fourth grader, so our Mythic Elephant was a small one. But Mrs. Smithee knew exactly how to hold her gray gloved arm next to her nose and wave it like an elephant would wave its trunk.

"Mrs. Smithee is here today in honor of Shambu. She will tell you all about Shambu, if you ask her," announced Mrs. Iptweet.

"Zack is our Mythic Dragon. Be sure to have a look at his tattoos. Excellent detail."

Zack flexed his arm muscles and made the dragons on his arms move around.

"The Queen of Beasts is here today. Zelda, you look lovely."

Zelda turned her back to us so everybody could see her lion tattoo. But Zelda did not flex any part of herself. Everybody clapped for Zack and Zelda.

"The Goddess of the Nile, Yolanda Ngoren, will be accompanying our kazooing with bongo drums. Yolanda, you look spectacular."

Yolanda did look truly spectacular. Her shiny red plastic high heel boots came up above her knees. Her boots went really well with her leopard-print top and her short red skirt.

Mrs. Iptweet said, "The peacock feathers in your braids, Yolanda, a brilliant idea."

"Thanks, Liz. I got me a cousin in Jersey with his own peacock farm."

Yolanda got a big round of applause from everybody.

Mrs. Iptweet turned her attention to the Mythic Fourth Graders.

"Our young Mythical Creatures are

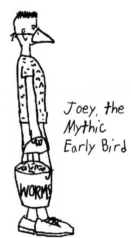

Joey, the Mythic Early Bird

from Mount Airy School. Joseph Zyweski is the Mythic Early Bird."

Clap, clap, clap. Yolanda checked out Joey's costume.

Yolanda said, "Is this a bunch of gummy worms pinned onto your shirt, Child? And your bucket is full of gummy worms, too? How about that. Do you know how much I like gummy worms?"

Joey kept looking at Yolanda's shiny red boots, probably because her boots were the same color as his shirt. Joey handed his bucket full of gummy worms to Yolanda.

Mythic Unicorn

Yolanda said, "I do not need all your gummy worms, Sonny. Not right now anyway. Just a couple is fine. Thanks."

Mrs. Iptweet kept going with the introducing, and we all kept clapping for each Mythical Creature.

"Kathleen McCullough is the elusive Unicorn. What a beautiful white dress, Kathleen. And your cone hat is perfect."

Clap, clap, clap.

"The Mythic Queen Bee is portrayed by Bea Bea Baldino."

Clap, clap, clap.

"The Frog Prince, Maximillion Steinberg. Good idea about the flippers, Max."

Clap, clap, clap.

"And representing the shadow side of the human mind, Isodore and Tomas Helsinki are the Loch Ness Monster. Well done, boys. Such an imaginative use of sheets and paint," said Mrs. Iptweet, "and the antlers are a nice touch."

Clap, clap, clap.

"We are fortunate today to have a real live member of the

avian community in our parade. Please welcome
Mrs. Romero and her parakeet Señora Puff o'
Fluff, who is portraying the Mythic Quetzalcoatl,
sacred bird of the Mayan people."

Quetzalcoatl

We gave the parakeet a big hand.

"Mrs. Romero, how did you get those long tail
feathers and headdress onto La Señora?"

"Oh, La Señora loves to dress up, Mrs. Iptweet,"
said Mrs. Romero. "And a person can do a lot these
days with the right craft supplies."

"Did you make the tiny purple cape yourself,
Mrs. Romero?"

"Oh, yes. I do enjoy sewing, Mrs. Iptweet, especially for my sweet little bird."

Then Mrs. Iptweet introduced herself, the Dove of Peace,
and me, the Mythic Storyteller, and the Mythic Wonder Horse
Pegasus, pinned onto my gold dress. Everybody clapped for us,
too.

Mrs. Iptweet leaned over and whispered in my ear, "Any sign
of your dad, Sheherazade?"

I whispered into Mrs. Iptweet's ear, "No, Mrs. Iptweet.
Probably he had an extremely important dance, wedding or parade to play in, at a place far away from here."

Mrs. Iptweet whispered back, "Let's hand out the parade
flags now. That will give him another minute, just in case he is
on his way."

I said, "Okay, Mrs. Iptweet."

On Thursday, only two days before the parade, Mrs. Iptweet
and I were pulling weeds, getting the garden ready for the parade, too. All of a sudden, Mrs. Iptweet stopped pulling a weed
and looked up. Her eyes were wide open.

"Flags," she said. "We need flags for the parade, Chérie."

The Loch Ness Monster

Mrs. Iptweet and I stopped everything. Mrs. Iptweet ran upstairs and raided her dish towel drawer. I was in charge of using Mrs. Iptweet's brightest yellow paint to make a large round sun with radiating rays on each light blue dish towel. Mrs. Iptweet hot-glued the painted dish towel flags onto her old mop handles. Mrs. Iptweet saves mop and broom handles for occasions just like this.

"You never know when you will need a nicely painted wooden stick, Chérie."

I said, "You are right about that, Mrs. Iptweet."

I handed out our parade flags to the Queen Bee, the Early Bird, and the Unicorn. We were all ready to go. There wasn't anything else to do but start parading around.

Mrs. Iptweet looked at me.

I said, "It's okay Mrs. Iptweet. Let's start the parade."

Mrs. Iptweet turned to our group of Mythical Creatures and announced, "It is time, Everyone. Let's begin."

We all walked to the end of the driveway.

"Big smiles! Good posture!" Mrs. Iptweet said.

We walked up the sidewalk of the busy street towards the end of our street.

"Remember to wave at anyone who might be here to watch our parade," said Mrs. Iptweet. "We show the spectators we appreciate them by waving at them and smiling!"

We were almost to the corner.

Mrs. Iptweet said, "The Mythic Storyteller, Sheherazade, will give the signal and we will start parading in honor of the longest day of the year."

The Mythical Creatures nodded their heads and said things like, "Okay!" and "Great!" and "Wow, here we go!"

At the corner, we stopped and I looked up our street. I got a big surprise. There were a lot of people standing around on the sidewalk. I wondered what happened on our street. Maybe there is a fire or an emergency, or a robbery has happened. Maybe everyone is waiting for the police or an ambulance or a fire truck to come.

I said, "Mrs. Iptweet, something has happened on Durham Street. Maybe we should we wait until the emergency is over and do the parade later."

Mrs. Iptweet took my hand and said, "Sheherazade, I think these people are here to watch our parade go by. I think what is happening is us."

What, I thought? Oh, no. The butterflies inside me went crazy. The sickening feeling in my stomach got really big. My legs froze. I felt faint.

Mrs. Iptweet said, "Breathe, Chérie. Stand tall. Smile."

Mrs. Iptweet squeezed my hand.

"It's time to give the signal, Sheherazade."

I breathed. I stood tall. I am tall for my age. I smiled a small smile. I turned around and faced all the Mythical Creatures.

I breathed in another big breath and used my loud voice to say, "And a-one, and a-two, and a-three."

Everyone put their kazoo in their mouth and started to hum *You are My Sunshine* almost all together. The Queen of the Nile joined in with her bongo drums. It sounded almost like a song. Mrs. Iptweet held my hand and we took the first step together up the sidewalk and began our parade.

CHAPTER EIGHTEEN

Parading Around

Small charming parades like our parade, parade on the sidewalk not the street because we do not want to get run over.
This means that we paraded close to the spectators of our parade. It was easy to wave and smile and shake hands and hug.

Mrs. Iptweet got hugged by two big tall guys standing in
front of her house.

"Nice going, Mom," they said.

Mrs. Iptweet said, "How sweet of you to be here. Oliver and
Finny, meet Sheherazade, the Mythic Storyteller."

I shook hands with Mrs. Iptweet's grown-up sons and said,
"Nice to meet you."

We kept walking up the street, and the parade spectators
made room for us to go by. People were smiling and pointing at
our costumes and saying things like, "What a good idea," and
"Who would believe this?"

Some people stood still with their hands on their hips, and their mouths not completely closed.

Some moms and dads and sisters and brothers of my fourth grader pals were there.

Bea Bea's dad yelled, "Woo hoo, you go, Queen Bee."

Joey's mom called out, "Stop eating the gummy worms off your shirt, Joey. NOW."

After a while I didn't need to hold Mrs. Iptweet's hand anymore. I walked and waved and kazooed, and looked at the people and smiled at them. Mostly I felt happy, but I had a small sadness wishing my dad was here, too, with his banjo, playing at my first parade. I decided to pay extra attention so I would not forget anything about this day. That way I could tell my dad everything exactly right the next time he takes me out to dinner.

At the end of the street we stopped and waited for the Mythic Mermaid and the Mythic Dragon and the Queen of

Queen of the Nile

Mythical Creatures

Me, waiting for my dad

Beasts to catch up. When all the Mythical Creatures were together again, Mrs. Iptweet said some words to everyone.

Sheherazade, the Mythic Storyteller

Probably she said something like "Well done, Everybody. Let's cross the street now and go down the other side."

But no one could hear her, not even me standing right next to Mrs. Iptweet, because an extremely loud noise was happening. A loud loud loud grumbling, like a monster dog growling, or the roar of a ferocious bear. The big sound sounded like my dad's motorcycle only even louder and noisier than usual.

Then, around the corner fast, came one, two, three motorcycles. Each motorcycle had a motorcycle driver man driving it. And each driver man had a banjo on his back. They stopped, one, two, three, right in the middle of the street in front of me and Mrs. Iptweet. I started to jump up and down. High-top sneakers are really good for jumping.

"Dad!" I yelled.

I ran out into the street to meet my dad.

My dad pulled off his helmet.

"Hey, Honeybun," he said.

He picked me up and gave me a big bear hug. I hugged him back really hard, so he would know I was so happy to see him. Then he set me back down onto the street and looked at me.

"That's a real nice dress, Honeybun," he said.

"Thanks, Dad. It's my Mythic Storyteller dress, Dad. Aunt Belle sent it to me in a suitcase envelope. I'm really glad you are here, Dad."

That's when my dad's motor-cycle friend spoke up.

"We would have been on time," he said, "but I had a flat. Sorry, Miss."

"Meet Carl and Harry," said my dad. "They're going to help out today. Unless we're too late, Honeybun."

"No way, Dad, you are not too late at all. We are only halfway done, Dad. Now we're going to walk down the other side of the street. This is my friend Mrs. Iptweet, Dad."

My dad climbed off his bike.

"Nice to meet you, ma'am."

My dad shook Mrs. Iptweet's hand and the hands of all the Mythical Creatures. Usually my dad wears black clothes, be-cause black clothes match his long black hair. But I saw that today my dad was wearing brown pants and a brown shirt and a fuzzy brown vest. When my dad was done shaking hands with all our paraders I said, "Dad, is this your ferocious terrifying Mythic Bear costume? It's pretty good, Dad."

My dad looked at me funny.

He bent down to whisper in my ear, "For everyone else, Honeybun, yeah. I'm a big scary bear." My dad looked around. "But for you, I'm a, um, um, you know, Honeybun."

A giggle popped out of me.

I whispered, "A teddy bear, Dad?"

"Don't tell anyone, okay?"

"Okay, Dad. No problem, Dad."

My dad gave me a thumbs-up. Then my dad stood up straight and tall. He swung his banjo around and strummed it. Banjos have a lot of sound in them.

Part of our parade of *Mythic Creatures*

"Mrs. Iptweet, what do you say we go down the middle of the street?" asked my dad.

"Well, Mr. Hornby, I am concerned about traffic that might come onto the street."

"No need to worry about that now, Mrs. Iptweet."

My dad nodded his head to Carl and Harry.

"Fellas," he said.

Carl and Harry roared down the street and parked their bikes at the other end, right in the middle of the street. My dad left his bike in the middle of the street at our end. It was a motorcycle blockade for our parade.

My dad strummed his banjo again. Carl and Harry ran up the street to meet us and strummed their banjos, too.

My dad said, "Let's roll."

So Mrs. Iptweet and I and all the Mythical Creatures paraded down the middle of Durham Street. Our three-banjo band playing behind us filled up all the air on Durham Street with big happy banjo sounds.

"This is wonderful, Chérie," said Mrs. Iptweet. "A real band for our parade."

The Dove of Peace

"Yeah, Mrs. Iptweet. I think the parade is turning out to be pretty good."

The parade spectators moved to the curb and into the street, and sat on the parked cars to see us. Some people opened their doors and came onto their porches to see what was going on. We did a lot of waving and smiling and kazooing and bongo-ing.

Then I heard my mom call out to me, "Yay, Storyteller!"

My mom was waving at me with both her arms in the air. I waved with both my hands at my mom. I smiled extra big so my mom could take a picture of me with her camera. My mom walked all along the street taking more and more pictures of me and all the paraders. Every part of me was full of music and waving and laughing.

After two times up and down the street, Mrs. Iptweet and I decided to end the parade right in front of the food tables. My face ached from so much smiling and my arms ached from so much waving, but I did not mind.

Right away, Mrs. Iptweet and I ate paper cups full of my mom's Divine Divinity. The gooey mixture of milk, pineapple, cherries, oranges, and marshmallows is the perfect food to eat after a parade.

Lots of people came up to us and said "Hey, good job, you two," and "I want to be in the parade next year," and "Where did you get the nerve?"

We kept saying, "Thank You," and "Sure," and "We were inspired, that's all."

Mrs. Iptweet and I watched and listened to everyone talk and visit and eat.

Mrs. Iptweet turned to me and said, "I think our parade is a success, Chérie. What do you think?"

I said, "Yes, Mrs. Iptweet. Our parade is definitely a success."

Mrs. Iptweet gave me a big hug and I hugged Mrs. Iptweet.

"You made a wonderful Mythic Storyteller, Chérie."

Mrs. Iptweet patted my head and pointed into the crowd.

"I see your dad looking for you, Zaddy Gal. Over there." Mrs. Iptweet squeezed my hand and said, "I'm going to help your mom and Mrs. Baldino and Ms. McKelvey with the food."

I said, "Okey Dokey, Mrs. Iptweet."

Then I yelled to my dad, "Hey, Dad, here I am!"

My dad found me in the crowd and picked me up and hugged me.

"Congratulations, Honeybun. This was a great parade."

I really like it when my dad picks me up. I hugged him really tight.

"Do you think so, Dad? I think so, too. Your banjo music is great, Dad. Thanks for playing at our parade, Dad." Some tears came into my eyes because a feeling of big happiness was filling up my whole body.

Then I thought my dad must be extremely hungry from all his playing and marching, just like I was.

I said, "Dad, we can sit together and eat right here on the curb, Dad. Isn't that a great idea, Dad? I'll make us plates of food."

"Okay, Honeybun. Sounds good to me."

I filled up one plate of food with four tamales, four pieces of fried chicken, two pieces of bread and butter, a mess of baked beans, big globs of potato salad and six corn muffins, all for my dad. Onto my plate I put four saucy chicken wings, celery sticks, a bluberry muffin, two tamales, a scoop of cheesy corn and peas, and Mythic Apple Salad with grapes.

When it was time for dessert I filled another plate with brownies, popcorn, and three pieces of Mrs. Iptweet's Coconut Cloud Cake, one for me, two for my dad. My dad and I ate and ate and talked about the parade and who was in it and the flat tire and what a close call it was.

Then I heard my mom's voice, "Hey you two, leave some room for my dessert."

My mom was balancing three bowls of Divine Divinity and three spoons in her hands. My dad got up to help my mom. My dad likes to be a gentleman to me and my mom. We all three settled back onto the curb and ate my mom's best special fancy food together.

"Thanks, Jane, this is really good. I have missed it," said my dad.

"You're welcome, Andrew," said my mom. My mom also said she was glad my dad could make it to the parade and I had worked so hard to pull it all together and she was proud of me.

"Yep, our Prudy is really something," said my dad. He mussed up my hair and slurped the last bit of Divine Divinity out of his bowl.

My mom let me stay up until the Midsummer sun went down. My mom and I watched the sky from our front porch until we saw the first star.

Then my mom said, "Okay, Darling Girl, up to bed with you. Let's go."

I was feeling pretty sleepy after such a long day of being

awake, so I said, "Okay, Mom. What a great and interesting day, huh, Mom?"

"Yes, it's been a great day, Prudy," said my mom. "I wouldn't have believed it if I hadn't seen it with my own eyes."

We walked up the stairs to my room.

I said, "Thanks for making so many bowls of Divine Divinity, Mom."

"No problem, Prudence. People seemed to like it."

"Mom, they loved it, Mom." We went into my room. "Did you like the parade, Mom?"

"Yes, Darling Girl. I did. It was fun. Where are your pajamas?"

"On my Dream-o-rama, Mom. Near the bottom rock. Maybe next year you would like to be in the parade, Mom."

My mom pulled my golden dress off over my head.

"We'll see, Darling Girl. I don't know if I'm much for marching in a parade."

"It was just regular walking, Mom. No marching at all. I wouldn't like to march either, Mom."

My mom pulled my pink nightgown on over my head. I put my arms into the armholes.

"Well, we'll see."

"What mythic animal would you be, Mom?"

"Climb into bed, Prudy. Probably a dolphin."

I climbed into my Dream-o-rama.

"Mom, that would be really great. You would make a great dolphin, Mom."

"Yes. Well, scootch under the covers, Prudy, and get settled. I have a surprise for you. I'll be right back."

My mom walked out of my room. I could hear her go into her room.

"What surprise, Mom?" I called out. "I already know that Dad is taking me to breakfast in the morning."

My mom came back into my room. In her hand she had a big book. It was Gran's big storybook.

"Mom, you said Gran's book was lost."

"It was lost. But now it is found. Move over a little bit, Prudy."

I was too tired to be shocked that my mom climbed into my Dream-o-rama next to me. She climbed right into the circle of creek rocks on my bed.

"I'm glad you found the book, Mom," I said.

"Which story would you like to hear, Prudy?"

"Whatever one you want, Mom. I like them all."

My mom paged through, then started to read. I could hear my mom's voice, and feel her warmth next to me. My eyes kept closing, but still my mind had some thoughts. What will I have for breakfast with my dad? Maybe pancakes. Or strawberry waffles. I will write to my Aunt Belle first thing in the morning. What will we use to make a dolphin costume for my mom next year? I know Mrs. Iptweet will have some ideas.

What will Mrs. Iptweet and I do for our next big project? The parade really happened. Isn't life amazing?

The End

How Mrs. Iptweet Got Her Name

Dear Reader,

I was just minding my own beeswax, living my life, when one night in 1996 or '97, I had a dream: I was riding on a bus. It was a boxy-shaped bus, clean and bright with large square windows. Two people were riding on the bus: myself, sitting in the very back seat, and another woman, who sat at the very front of the bus. She had dark hair and was wearing a pale lavender-colored dress. After a while, the bus came to a stop, the door opened and onto the bus climbed a young girl. She was about 8 years old, maybe 9. She had long brown hair and bangs. She was wearing a dress, too. I saw her notice the woman in the front and then take a seat right across the aisle from her. The girl did not notice me at all but she kept turning to stare at the woman. After a lot of staring, the girl stood up and stepped into the aisle in front of the woman and said, "You're the lady who tells the stories, aren't you?"

The woman turned to her – I could see her face now and it was a lovely face, but a little bit sad it seemed to me. She said to the girl in a quiet, friendly voice, "Yes, I am." And smiled.

Then, in the way of dreams, the lady turned to look at me sitting all the way in the back of the bus and the next thing I know her face is right in front of me and she looks me straight in the eye, deep deep into my eyes, and says, "My name is Mrs. Iptweet. That's I-P-T-W-E-E-T." She spelled her name one more time. Then I woke up. And wrote it down.

Barbara Mayfield
Glorieta, February 2009